The rebar industry is not for the faint at heart . . .

Looking past Austin's strained face, Tillie saw his right arm raised upward with his hand around the rope that had previously draped across the chasm. He had caught it as they fell and now clutched it in a tenuous grip. Even as she watched, the rope slipped, and his fingers slid agonizingly down the rough fibers. Holding her as he was, it was impossible to secure his grip by wrapping the rope around his hand, and the lifeline continued its slow crawl from Austin's grasp.

Through clenched teeth, he grunted, "Grab the rope!"

Caught between obedience and the fear of tearing herself from Austin's hold, Tillie felt for the loose end and closed first one hand and then the other around it. At her nod, he released her long enough to improve his own grip.

Would the dirt embankment give way and swallow them up, buried alive? Tillie wondered desperately. *What secured the rope they clung to?*

MARY CARPENTER REID is a prolific author who writes for both adults and children. Her recent novels, *Topatopa* and *Dressed for Danger*, part of the popular Citrus County Mystery Series, further established her as an inspirational romance writer. Mrs. Reid and her husband reside in Brea, California.

Books by Mary Carpenter Reid

CITRUS COUNTY MYSTERY SERIES—TWO BOOKS IN ONE

CCMC1—Topatopa & Dressed for Danger

Rebar

Mary Carpenter Reid

Heartsong Presents

ISBN 1-55748-365-5

REBAR

PRINTED IN U.S.A.

one

Tillie Gibson, blessed with two healthy parents and numerous robust friends, had attended only one funeral in her twenty-seven years, until today. As the black limousine returned her to her aunt Dee's house on a bright Saturday afternoon incredibly free of southern California smog, she wondered if the somber driver had misunderstood his instructions.

Surely he had come that morning to the wrong address. Surely he had driven the wrong family in that tedious procession led by a black hearse. Somewhere, another family still waited patiently for this driver, waited to caress a silver casket in a final touch of love.

People would realize the dreadful mistake that had been made if only her uncle Wallace would come striding from the orchard behind the house. In his work-roughened hands, he'd carry newly picked grapefruit, fragrant and heavy with juice, and he'd inquire where everyone had been.

But that was impossible.

Instead, the intense odor of gardenia blossoms in an enormous spray of white flowers assaulted Tillie, tugging her back to unwelcome reality. The arrangement had arrived too late for the funeral and hung from a tripod near Dee's front door. A shimmering silver ribbon read, "Ironclad Friends."

She wanted to throw this tardy offering from the narrow porch of the stucco house, but disposing of a white funeral spray wouldn't change the fact that Wallace Kombardy had departed this world to be with the Lord, and she and Dee were left to mourn.

A torrent of grief shook Tillie. *I go now to prepare a place for you.* At the graveside, the pastor had spoken of that promise by Jesus. She grasped at the thought and repeated it over and over to herself. Yes, Jesus had prepared a place for Wallace.

From behind Tillie, a masculine voice rattled the peace of mind she had managed at last to claim.

"Here, I'll open the door."

She shrank from the hand that circled around her to turn the knob, allowing her eyes to roam no farther than the white sliver of shirt cuff that peeked beneath the dark suit sleeve. At this moment, her shredded emotions simply could not deal with Austin Neff.

Inside the sprawling ranch-style house, built in Brogerston in the 1950s when Citrus County land was plentiful, the smell of baked ham replaced the fragrance of gardenias. Friends from Dee's hospital auxiliary worked in the kitchen, preparing a buffet for the carloads of people that zigzagged into parking spaces on the tree-shaded street.

The guests hung back respectfully, allowing the family a chance to regain their composure. Soon the Kombardy home balanced on that clumsy threshold between memorial service and party. In a black flowing dress, enthroned on a flowered chintz-covered chair in the living room, Dee responded gracefully to the stream of people passing by. From time to time, she took off her glasses and pressed a white linen hanky to her red-rimmed eyes.

Gradually, hushed conversation gave way to uneasy socializing. Women discussed wallpaper and how young Dee looked. Men talked about the new county sales tax and the weather.

A neighbor pressed Tillie's arm. "Too bad your mother and father couldn't return to the States for the services."

Another scoffed at such an idea. "But her father works in that

North African country." She addressed Tillie, "Your aunt understands that it would have been too long a trip for them to make for her husband's funeral. Besides, she has you and her son to help her."

Tillie nodded.

"And, it's not like Wallace Kombardy was a true blood relative of you and your folks. Goodness knows, no one would guess that he was, with him being so burly and you being so delicate looking."

A third woman, one Tillie didn't recognize, joined the discussion. "His first wife was your mother's sister, wasn't she?"

"Yes, my aunt. . . ."

"I remember her, your mother's sister. Had brown eyes, like yours, and dark blond hair too. Only she didn't have those streaks of honey brown running through like you do. Seems only yesterday that we gathered here in this very room after her funeral."

The first neighbor frowned at the newcomer. "That was a long time ago." She brightened. "And a few years later, we were all so happy when Wallace found Dee."

The second woman's fingers flexed, counting time. "Wallace and Dee married while you were still in high school, isn't that right, Tillie? I remember when your folks left the country and you came here to live."

Helplessly wedged in the tight triangle of well-meaning women, Tillie nodded.

"Well," said the first, "now Dee will reap the rewards of that kindness. You'll be such a comfort."

Tillie cringed at the inference that the Kombardys had taken her in as some sort of waif. It hadn't been that way at all. An auxiliary member, peering from the kitchen with an anxious look on her face, gave Tillie the excuse she needed. "Pardon me, I think someone has a question."

She sidled away with the conversation following her. "Don't forget Dee's son. Austin has settled into the guest house this time. Almost providential the way he arrived before the accident."

"Terrible accident. My husband's barber saw the car Wednesday night being towed, what was left of it, that is."

"Now Austin can stay and run the business for his mother."

Tillie hurried to put more distance between herself and the neighbor women. She feared that next might come a rehash of events with Dee's son the summer after her college graduation. Some of these people would remember.

From her place on the chintz-covered chair, Dee met Tillie's glance. The widow's hand lifted in a fluttering motion that Tillie interpreted as a sign of survival. Reassured, Tillie continued toward the kitchen.

A chain of three coatless men, Kombardee Steel employees, met her near the dining room. They carried hearty plates of food on their way to join more ironworkers gathered in the side yard.

"Thanks for coming, Bob," she told the first man. "It means a lot to me, and to Mrs. Kombardy." She moved to the next. "Thanks, Steve. I appreciate this."

The third acted as spokesperson. "Mr. Kombardy was the best...," he stifled an adjective that might have offended Tillie, "boss in the rebar business. Everybody thought so, even the men who don't work at Kombardee anymore."

Anxious to be on their way outside, they moved toward the door as one man added, "And no hard feelings by them either."

That last statement puzzled Tillie only momentarily. Ralph Delanoy, his kind eyes shielded behind dark-rimmed glasses, was waiting to claim Tillie's attention. "Didn't get to speak to you at the service."

The attorney, a long-time friend of her uncle, enfolded Tillie in a gentle hug. His voice cracked with emotion. "I'll never see another fishing season open without thinking of the great times your uncle and I had tromping along those Sierra trout streams."

She manufactured a smile and pushed herself away, vigorously brushing at the wrinkle she'd put in his silk tie. He and Wallace had remained friends for decades, even though this man had become a respected member of the bar and Wallace ran a blue-collar operation. "My uncle never tired of telling stories about your escapades."

"This last spring was the first opening I remember him missing. Wasn't the same without him. Mack Swazee and the other fellows said the same thing. We had good times together."

One of Dee's friends pressed a plate of food on Tillie. The pink ham slice and creamy potato salad together with crisp raw vegetables and roll were arranged in an attractive pattern, a perfect picture, typical of what one would expect of her aunt's genteel friends. Tillie had not been hungry for three days since she'd received that terrible telephone call. People had constantly offered food and drink as if that would ease the pain of losing a person who had been almost as dear to her as her own father.

"You really must eat a little." A pink acrylic nail pointed to the plate. "To keep up your strength. Come, let's find you a place to sit." One smooth hand carried the plate while the other guided Tillie by the elbow toward a chair offered by a gray-haired woman Tillie thought might be in Dee's exercise class.

Ralph Delanoy leaned over Tillie and whispered, "I need to talk with you in private."

But the gray-haired woman had condolences to offer. "Dee has told me how close you were to your uncle. She always admired the way you worked with him. She's often said that you could run the business yourself if need be." The woman smiled at her overstatement.

Another member of Dee's exercise group pulled up a chair. "Thank goodness Dee has a son." She giggled in a squeaky sort of way. "He'll fit into a steel company better than a, er, gentle-looking person like you."

Tillie wished she could say what she felt. *Austin may have the physical qualifications, but he's never shown any serious interest in Kombardee Steel.*

"You have a retail shop, don't you? European lace?"

"Not yet," Tillie corrected. "I work at Malverns. I hope to open a shop someday and carry heirloom-type merchandise."

"Oh," the woman trilled, "I love beautiful linens and bedding."

"That, and also gift and decorative items with a Victorian flavor."

"I can just see it. . . dark wooden flooring, lace scarves draped over antique tables, glass-fronted display cabinets," the gray-haired woman observed. "Quite a contrast to your uncle's business. Exactly what kind of steel did he make?"

"Uncle Wallace didn't make steel. Kombardee Steel is a rebar company. Actually, the professional publications call them rebars. We usually just say rebar."

"Oh?"

"You know those metal bars that are put down before concrete is poured? Those are steel reinforcing rods." Tillie cut a bite of ham. "To reinforce the concrete."

"Like in a patio?"

"Right. Kombardee Steel fabs and places rebar, that is, our shop cuts and bends reinforcing steel to the correct dimensions and shape. Then the field crews put it into place on the job site." Tillie decided not to mention the wire mesh sometimes used.

She pierced a chunk of fresh orange with a plastic fork and put it in her mouth to counter the salty ham taste.

"Oh, Dee's company builds patios?"

"More like the framework for concrete structures. Usually buildings or parking garages. Sometimes drainage channels and culverts."

"But they call it a steel company?"

"In a generic sort of way."

"Well, whatever," the woman summarized. "Dee owns a company. How nice."

That conversation spent, Tillie said, "Excuse me, I need a glass of water."

"Let me bring you one," volunteered a passerby.

"No, I'll get it." Tillie jumped up, but immediately encountered Esther Vargas, office manager at Kombardee Steel. They had spoken earlier. Now they stood face to face, awkwardly repeating a little of their previous exchange.

"Your aunt appears to be holding up well." Esther smoothed her hair back, an unnecessary gesture considering her hairstyle. Her severe, tightly held bun was softened only slightly by small clusters of ringlets that bounced deliberately around her ears. Her natural graying black color was well disguised with red dye, but nothing hid the fact that Esther was well into her fifties.

"It seems that way."

The exercise class continued their conversation, probably not realizing that Tillie was within hearing. "One blessing, Dee is well fixed."

"A steel company," marveled another. "She may have lost a husband, but she'll be more than comfortable the rest of her life."

"There's bound to be insurance too."

Tillie's stomach went into a tailspin. She redoubled her

efforts to get away, but found herself jostling for space with Esther Vargas, who also seemed anxious to be someplace else. The set to the woman's chin and the full lips compressed into a thin red line caused Tillie to wonder if the careless remarks made the office manager as uneasy as Tillie.

Esther's eyes darted past Tillie to the front hall and she pushed off in that direction, lemonade sloshing from the glass in her hand. A moist trail on Dee's carpet, the tell-tale evidence of Esther's agitated state, was soon covered over by the room's shifting occupants.

From time to time, as the afternoon wore on and the mourners drifted away, Ralph Delanoy approached Tillie. But always another claimed her attention. Finally, he took her arm and guided her to the den adjoining the living room. Dee was already there, huddled in the occasional chair opposite the handsome desk she had presented to her husband the previous Christmas. After closing the louvered double doors, Ralph escorted Tillie to the companion chair, adjusted the blinds against a flood of late afternoon sun, and took his place behind the desk.

"This won't take long. And don't worry, it isn't any sort of formal reading of the will as we've all seen in the movies."

Tillie reached over and patted Dee's slender arm, which seemed to have grown thinner the past few days. For Dee's sake, Tillie wished that legal matters concerning Wallace's estate could be delayed. How much longer could her aunt maintain this robotlike calmness? The black silk dress Dee wore seemed to accentuate her alarming pallor. She looked ready to faint.

Ralph cleared his throat. "You know how I felt about your husband, Dee. None of us is over the shock of his unexpected death."

Dee leaned heavily on the chair arms.

"As you're aware, Wallace asked me years ago to act as executor of his estate."

Dee nodded. Tillie remembered mention of it; she would have assumed it anyway.

"I've already done much of what is necessary. I do need signatures on several things. I wouldn't ask you today except that, unfortunately, I have to catch a flight to Europe in a few hours." He begged for understanding. "I apologize for being gone at a time like this, but it's a commitment I accepted long ago."

Dee murmured, "That's all right, Ralph."

"I'll be back in Citrus County week after next. In the meantime, if you have questions, call the office and ask for my nephew."

"What's your nephew's name?"

The politely direct question came from behind Tillie. Startled, she twisted in her chair and saw a fourth person in the room.

"My nephew is David Delanoy," the attorney answered the man who leaned against the wall near the louvered doors. "Austin joined us," said Ralph, stating the obvious.

"Of course." Tillie quickly turned back to the desk. To her it was only natural that Dee's son be present for legal conferences.

Dee asked Tillie, "You don't mind that Austin is here?"

"Oh, no, not at all. He can be of more help to you if he knows what is going on."

"If only I had gone to the office once in a while. I feel so lost. I'm relying on you, Tillie. You know everything about Wallace's company, and I don't know anything. Now I'm left with his company to run. A steel company!"

"Remember, it's been over a year since I worked at the office steadily. But whatever I can do. . . ."

"Thank goodness Austin came back when he did. He's been putting in long hours for weeks."

Ralph Delanoy placed a multipage document in front of Dee and offered a pen. At her pitifully bewildered expression, he assured her, "You have my word that it's all right to sign whatever I hand you today. Of course, take time to read anything you wish."

Dee scanned the pages, looked over her shoulder at Austin, and then scrawled her signature where the attorney pointed. She did the same for the next document and the next.

As she did, Ralph passed them to Tillie. "Your signature, too, Tillie."

She complied without question, being accustomed to signing documents occasionally at Ralph Delanoy's direction. She'd held the title of chief financial officer at Kombardee Steel for years, but it was for legal rather than practical purposes.

Satisfied, Ralph said, "There, that gives you authority to act in Wallace's place."

Dee moaned. "Whatever will I do?" She looked first at Tillie and then back at Austin.

A flicker of alarm upset Ralph Delanoy's orderly demeanor. Quickly, he set the record straight. "I meant Tillie. Tillie will act in Wallace's place."

Tillie gasped. Dee jerked upright with a tiny cry.

The attorney rushed to explain. "I supposed you both knew. Wallace left his company to the two people he loved most. The arrangements he made are really for the best, really to your advantage, Dee."

Tillie probed, "What did you mean, that I'd be acting in his place?"

Ralph Delanoy tapped his pen smartly on the paper desk pad. "I'm sure that Wallace intended to tell you both." The pen pecked away at the pad, twirling from end to end.

"Tell them what?" Austin moved forward, but not quite into the circle around the desk.

The attorney's patient answer was one of a man treading lightly. "Tillie has always shared in the ownership of the company by virtue of a small number of shares. However, Wallace recently made some changes in his will that, with his death, substantially increase Tillie's ownership."

"To—to what?" Tillie stammered.

The sun had ceased glaring through the blinds. The attorney switched on Wallace's brass desk lamp. "To fifty-one percent. Dee will hold title to the other forty-nine percent. You see," he leaned forward earnestly, "Wallace wanted to turn ownership of his company over to a person who would—and could—take care of the company, someone to operate it in such a way that it will generate income for both you and Dee."

"Operate it?" Tillie heard herself ask.

Dee babbled, "But Tillie wants to sell linens with lace trim and blouses with lace collars and cutwork. She doesn't want to traipse around construction sites."

"Now, Dee. This doesn't mean that Tillie has to wear a hard hat the rest of her life. Wallace knew all about Tillie's ambition for a 'frilly shop,' as he called it. But he'd begun to have some real fears about the future of the business if he were to die suddenly."

"Which he did," Dee began to sob.

"So," Ralph continued, "he decided to make Tillie majority stockholder. He trusted her to act in the best interests of you and the company." The attorney addressed Tillie solemnly. "That's quite a trust, to will you controlling interest in a company he spent his life building. In effect, young lady, you own Kombardee Steel."

"But shouldn't his wife be the owner?" Tillie asked.

Dee dabbed at her eyes. "Wallace was always logical about his decisions. He knew Tillie could do a good job with his company. She knows everything, even more than Austin, I guess."

At the mention of Austin, a chill seeped through the state of shock that surrounded Tillie. Austin would have expected, as almost everyone, that his mother inherited control of Kombardee Steel. Austin would be expected to run the company for his mother.

Ralph Delanoy removed himself from any potential disagreements. "My job is to carry out my client's wishes."

In a daze, Tillie continued signing the documents the attorney put in front of her. She paused between signatures and smoothed her hand over her skirt to dry her moist fingers.

Finally, Ralph Delanoy snapped his briefcase shut. "I have to catch that plane. Tillie, you'll need the set of papers I'm leaving on the desk. There are more formalities, but we've covered enough that you can now act as president."

Dee asked meekly, "Do you mind. . . being president?"

Tillie opened her mouth, but couldn't come up with an answer.

Ralph patted Tillie's shoulder and kissed Dee's forehead. "I'll let myself out." He stopped for a brief handshake with Austin, then opened the doors to the now deserted living room. Muffled kitchen sounds indicated that Dee's faithful friends were cleaning up.

The brass lamp shed a lonely spot of light on Wallace's empty desk. Tillie eased out of her chair and down on her knees. She put an arm around Dee's waist and leaned her head against the older woman's thin, black-clad shoulder.

Austin's voice breached the uneasy silence. "President Tillie Gibson."

His words, filled with undisguised surprise and tinged with skepticism, confirmed what Tillie already sensed. Not many people were going to see the logic of Wallace's decision to turn the reins of his beloved company over to a twenty-seven-year-old niece who wanted to buy and sell lace, not steel. She hugged Dee even harder.

Austin drifted away. Tillie heard the front door close and sighed, thankful that he was gone.

two

Monday morning Tillie noticed something odd the moment her car approached the entrance to Kombardee Steel. At nine a.m., the gate in the chain-link fence surrounding the three-acre property was still rolled across the drive leading to the office. It should have been opened two hours earlier. Fortunately, the second gate, down the road and used mostly by trucks, was open. Tillie had a handful of keys, but she'd never needed one for the gate.

She had spent a painful Sunday afternoon with Dee, partly to keep her company but also to quiz her on company matters. Austin had disappeared; according to his mother, he had gone to a friend's. Tillie would have to be more desperate than she was before she would ask him anything.

She turned her white Ford into the far gate and had no trouble finding a parking spot for the two-door. Where were the usual cars and pickups that lined the spaces in front of the one-story office building? The few vehicles here hardly represented enough employees to run the office and shop, to say nothing of customers or vendors who might be expected on a Monday morning. She recognized Esther Vargas's blue Buick four-door with its new paint job.

A pickup roared out from the yard behind the shop. The driver slammed on his brakes and leaned out the truck window, obviously annoyed. He yelled toward Tillie, "Got a message for your boss."

The only thing familiar about the man was his major league baseball cap.

"Tell him this is the last time I'm coming here for steel. I'm sick of wasting a trip. You don't carry enough inventory to bother looking at."

With that, the tires squealed and gravel spit in all directions in the driver's haste to leave.

Instead of going into the office, Tillie walked to the right, between the big shop building and the road. The shop consisted of some loosely connected covered areas and sheds. Most of the shop, however, was out in the open. This allowed for movement of sixty-foot lengths of rods brought from the yard to be cut and bent to specifications for Kombardee jobs. A bender and noisy shear line were in operation, doing just that.

Tillie asked Jim, a shop employee, to remind the foreman to open the main gate. Then she continued along the front of the property to where she could view the wide space between the shop area and the side fence. She hadn't taken a good look at the yard for months. Normally, huge quantities of steel and mesh were stored on dunnage in neat rows extending nearly to the rear fence.

A sizeable number of small customers, laying their own steel, regularly bought reinforcing rods and wire mesh from Kombardee. But the angry man in the baseball cap had been right. The stock was reduced to a deplorable size.

Discouraged at being handed problems before she'd even crossed the office threshold, Tillie headed for the one-story office building. She frowned at the sight of the small patch of brown, ill-kept grass on either side of the walk leading to the main office door. She'd remarked at its dryness the last time she spent a Saturday here with Wallace. He'd passed it off using the California rationale, "Haven't you heard? There's no brown grass in this state, only golden."

With a pang of guilt, Tillie counted back and realized that

more than a month had elapsed since that Saturday. A surge of overtime in her own job at Malverns in Tarfield had kept her busy. Then she'd taken those few days up the coast with a friend, visiting specialty shops, tucking away ideas for her own dream.

Tillie carefully avoided touching the green wreath tied with a black ribbon that hung on the office door. A rush of emotion swept over her as she stepped into the reception area, a ten-square-foot area partially cordoned from the rest of the room by straight chairs.

Esther Vargas occupied her customary place, the first desk on the right. A phone propped on her shoulder, the office manager greeted Tillie with a tilt of the head and continued her conversation, obviously having a communication problem with a temporary employment agency. She put down the phone and puffed a sigh of disgust. "We need help, not arguments."

The office looked in need of help. A thorough cleaning would have been a start. Tillie didn't remember it ever appearing so untidy. But she held her tongue, thinking that criticism of that sort wouldn't improve Esther's mood.

She moved a stray wastebasket from the center aisle and retreated to her unofficial desk, opposite Esther's, that was reserved for her use on the days she helped out, usually Saturdays. Two more desks stood cluttered but unoccupied in the other corners of the room. Filing cabinets, tables, and extra chairs filled in the cracks.

Another call came in and Esther answered in her resounding voice. Tillie pointed to the two desks that looked as if they'd been carelessly abandoned in the middle of a work day. "Where is everybody?"

Esther lifted her eyebrows helplessly and talked louder into the mouthpiece. The conversation gave signs of being an extended one.

This main office was an open area except for a single shoulder-high partition that jutted out from the wall by Esther's desk. It and the wall behind gave the office manager a semblance of privacy. The aura of status was thin since there was little privacy to be had with the glass windows lining the entire office front. Besides, every person entering the door would naturally stop at her desk.

Tillie dropped her purse in a drawer of the desk and set her briefcase on the floor. She answered another call.

A woman identified herself, naming a company Tillie knew to be a small general contractor. She asked for the office manager. "She's on another line. This is Tillie Gibson. Can I help you?"

"You're installing steel for a job we're doing in the new industrial park over on Acacia Avenue." It seemed more accusation than statement. "You people are holding us up. My job superintendent says your crew is there but we can't let them work without a signed contract." Pent-up exasperation poured out. "I warned some man in your office last week that the original we received wasn't signed and somebody would have to get us one that was."

Tillie knew this contractor handled drives and block walls, jobs smaller than the ones Kombardee usually bid. "Let me check on that. I'll call you right back."

"I'll hold. This is costing us money, you know."

An idle crew parked at a job site was costing Kombardee money too. Esther was still tied up on the phone. Tillie located the job folder and thumbed through it, at last procuring the contract agreement. Vexed, she saw that the signature line under Kombardee Steel was blank.

"Esther," she asked demandingly, "do you know anything about the contract for the industrial park on Acacia?"

Esther shook her head. "Nothing special. Why?"

"The contractor's office claims they don't have a signed contract." She held out their own unsigned copy.

Esther frowned. "I do remember some fuss about it. It came back. What with all the commotion about your uncle getting a fax machine, maybe it got sent out a second time still blank."

"What's a fax got to do with this?"

"That's what your uncle said. So we didn't buy one. He told Puckatt that important papers had to be original anyway." She screwed her mouth sideways and looked up at the ceiling.

Tillie waited while Esther searched her memory.

"Maybe somebody was going to hand-deliver it, I don't know."

"Who?"

"Could have been Puckatt."

Tillie returned to her desk. Esther Vargas never minded a dig at poor John Puckatt, the operations manager. She picked up the phone and this time was greeted with an entirely different attitude from the construction company office.

"Sorry if I sounded a little ragged," the woman said. "I just this moment heard about Mr. Kombardy. You're his niece, aren't you?"

Tillie affirmed that she was. "I'll have the signed contract to your office in thirty minutes."

The woman wasn't finished explaining the tongue-lashing she'd given Tillie. "It's just that this same sort of thing has happened once or twice before."

"Well, it won't happen again."

Tillie asked Esther to find somebody to deliver the contract and decided she should check the two unoccupied desks for more obvious oversights. When Esther came back, Tillie asked, "Where are these people?"

One desk had a nameplate. Esther indicated the other. "That's been an unpopular desk. The last person stayed two days. I can't remember her name. I'll look in the file if you want."

"Two days?"

"She was from the temp agency. Let's see, the one before her left on vacation and never returned."

"Goodness, Esther. What have you been doing to our employees?" Tillie hoped she sounded more easygoing than she felt.

"It's not me," Esther said emphatically. Her eyes wandered toward the back of the building.

"What about Janice?" Tillie read the nameplate on the last desk. "She was hired several months ago, wasn't she?"

"I suppose. She wasn't the type to work on Saturdays when you were likely be here."

Tillie didn't mention that Esther never worked Saturdays either, and there would have been a revolt if it had ever been required. Wallace had tried not to ask employees to give up weekends.

"Anyway," Esther continued, "Janice called in sick Tuesday, and I haven't heard from her since."

"Has anybody contacted her?"

"Too busy, what with. . . ."

Tillie nodded. "I'll do it myself."

Esther answered another call and told Tillie, "This man wants to speak to our purchasing agent. About stationery. I'll tell him we don't need anything."

Tillie bit her lip. She would have to think about a new letterhead. "Tell him to contact me next week. And, Esther, I'll take all general calls for the office, except those you normally handle."

Soon Esther was back on the phone. "Yes, we're devastated about Mr. Kombardy's passing. Just a minute, please." She put her hand over the mouthpiece. "What shall I say when they ask who is taking your uncle's place and are we still in business?"

Tillie returned to the desk she always used, sat down, and clasped her hands firmly in front of her. "Of course, we are still in business. Tell them Tillie Gibson is the new president."

Esther accepted the announcement with an explosion of expression but no outcry. She kept the caller waiting long enough to observe to Tillie, "Well, most people would think a girl like you couldn't run the place, but I know better." She enlightened the person on the other end of the line, hung up, and said, "He wanted to know how to address a letter. By the way, who is the new operations manager?"

"Why, whoever took over after John Puckatt retired."

"That was just a week ago last Friday. Wallace never said who it would be."

"What?"

Esther shrugged as if it didn't matter. "Austin has been spending a lot of time in the office, and he's always using Puckatt's phone. Sometimes I've referred people to him. He might as well be it, except. . . ."

Tillie waited.

"Except your uncle. . . ."

"My uncle what?"

Esther grabbed a handful of papers. "I gotta make copies. That state inspector will be on my back if I don't do something about these new safety rules." She marched to the copy machine.

Dumbfounded, Tillie gave up. Esther's most annoying habit was to hint at something she might or might not know anything about and then clam up. But how in the world did Wallace expect the company to function without an operations manager, especially when the office was understaffed? She followed the center aisle between the desks to the back office. She should check on whether or not the physical facilities had disappeared along with the employees.

The aisle turned into a hallway. On the right, a closed door led to Wallace's office. She would investigate that later. Beyond it was a small office for the operations manager, empty of both John Puckatt and his precious Porsche scale model usually displayed on his desk, a replica of his own black Porsche. The rumpled cover of a personal finance magazine peeked from the dozen or so telephone books stacked in a corner.

Beyond this office estimators worked in a large room. On the left was an even larger room filled with drafting tables and stools, desks and tables, and a blueprint machine. This was the home of Kombardee's detailers and design engineers. Tillie waved to the few men there.

"Good to see you, Tillie," one said. The first-name policy had always been standard practice at Kombardee.

"Thanks." She moved on quickly, knowing that she should compose a statement to the employees. They deserved to know the status of the company and their jobs and who they were working for. Further, she needed to get out a news release and a letter to customers. What about thank-you letters from the company to the businesses that had sent expressions of sympathy? All that was in addition to getting down to work.

She glanced in a small general office used by whatever person needed space at the moment. It was empty. She returned to the front office to the niche carved in the back wall that contained what Esther grandly called the wet bar. To Esther's consternation, Wallace had called it the kitchen. It did have a sink, toaster, an old-model microwave, and even a small refrigerator. Everyone else simply referred to it by its most important appliance, the coffee machine.

Reinforced with a cup of coffee, she approached the closed door of her uncle's office. She pulled out the key, conspicuously shiny in its newness; Wallace had only recently installed a lock on his office door. Making a hollow sound, the key flopped over too easily. The door swung inward. A sudden motion near Wallace's desk confirmed Tillie's suspicion: The door had already been unlocked. Austin Neff whirled to face her. In a knee-jerk reaction, she spilled hot coffee over her fingers.

The ceiling lights were off. The sun coming through the window softened the freckles that dotted the sides of Austin's face, blending them into tan. He hadn't been around iron long enough to bear the missing fingertips and scars of many men in this business, but he had enough rough edges to make him seem at home in an outdoor setting. That was especially true when he wore an Aussie-type unbleached muslin hat and snapped one side of the wide brim up to the crown. Like today.

Austin spoke first. "I was checking to see if I might be able to take care of anything here. Didn't know when you'd be in."

"Oh," she said in a nonanswer.

Behind him, as if pushed by an unseen hand, an old ledger slid from its perch on a stack of file folders at the corner of the desk. Wallace had used that one for years and had kept right on using it even after the first computer appeared on the premises.

Austin hastily picked it up and repositioned it. Tillie closed the door and walked around behind the desk. She cleared a spot for her coffee cup. Pulling a tissue from her pocket, she methodically wiped her fingers and then folded the brown-stained tissue into a precise square.

As she dropped it in a wastebasket, she caught sight of the

half-opened lower drawer where the ledger was sometimes kept when it wasn't in the safe. The safe, in the wall behind an oil painting depicting the nearby mountain range, was the company's worst-kept secret. Always unlocked, the safe served as protection from fire, not thieves.

Austin defused her unspoken question. "Lots of things out of place. You have quite a job ahead of you."

Would she ever again feel at ease with this man? she wondered absently. "Nobody knows that better than I."

He removed his hat and brushed back a shock of sun-bleached brown hair. "Congratulations on your new title."

She dredged up an artificial chuckle. "What do you do around here anyway?"

With humility that didn't fit the Austin she knew, he answered, "Me? A little of this and a little of that. General flunky, as the saying goes."

Tillie knew this flunky had graduated with honors from a midwestern university. He'd worked as a geologist since the winter after her own college graduation. But she went along with his pretense. "Taking a sabbatical from your job?"

"You could call it that."

"Well, it's nice for your mother that you happened to be here when. . . when. . . ."

He supplied what she couldn't say. "When her husband died. Yes, and I haven't had an opportunity to properly tell you, Tillie. . . ."

No one else had ever said her name that way, with a lilt, almost a musical inflection. But no one else had his low, warm, husky voice.

". . . I'm sorry about your Uncle Wallace. I know how close you were, and I can only guess how much you'll miss him."

"Your mother will miss him too."

Austin sighed. "I know."

"Their anniversary was coming up. They were so happy. I loved my real aunt when she was alive, but I love Aunt Dee, too, and she was good for Uncle Wallace."

Austin agreed. "She certainly was. She's generous to a fault."

As Tillie wondered at the strangeness of that remark, he added, "With her emotions, I mean."

She nodded. "Our only consolation is that the separation is temporary. Dee and I both know we'll all be together again. . . ."

"Yes, yes." Austin seemed anxious to end the meeting. "I have to get out to the shop." He was almost to the door when he turned and stalked back. "I mean it, I am sorry that your uncle is gone. I want to offer my help here. I've been around enough summers that I have a smattering of experience in almost everything related to this business. Your uncle had me in the field plenty of times." A twinkle warmed his blue eyes. "I still think the damage is permanent from carrying bundles of steel one summer." He rubbed his right shoulder and dropped it in at an exaggerated angle. "Do I look like I'm walking on the side of a mountain?"

This time Tillie's chuckle was real. "And the following year you were supposed to learn estimating. Uncle Wallace never gave up on you. That was the summer that we rode bikes to the beach. . . ."

"Two or three times a week."

Suddenly they had followed the memories too far, to a time better forgotten.

A red flush crept up from Austin's open shirt collar. "Maybe your uncle should have given up on me before. . . maybe that way no one would have gotten hurt."

She looked away reluctantly.

He started back to the door. "The offer still stands. I do have a fair idea of what it takes to run this place. Of course, you know it inside and out, far better than I."

She drew a finger along the edge of a nearby table top, cutting through the dust that covered it. "How long do you plan to stay this time?"

"Depends. I've been thinking of maybe branching out on my own, consulting. Nothing definite yet. Lots of opportunities in this area."

That could explain why he'd shown up and why he'd moved into the guest house. "Yes," she said, proud of how cool she sounded, "Citrus County is teeming with career opportunities. Probably needs geologists. Oil and building, stuff like that."

"Besides, my mother could use the companionship for a while. Help her over the rough spots."

He left, closing the door after himself. She sat at Wallace's desk, her head in her hands.

The enormity of her responsibility began to seep through the wall she had erected the night of the accident, the wall that kept her emotions under control and all the hideous unknowns at bay. The thought of making sense from the mounds of papers strewn on the desk top like pages torn from a thousand books and stirred in a reckless circle was overwhelming. She'd been cast into the role not only of leading the company but of salvaging order from neglect. *What had happened to Uncle Wallace?* she thought for the umpteenth time. Sure, she'd noticed a change in him. But how could everything slide so far downhill in the month since she had last been there? Or had the slide begun long before?

She eased her head down to the desk. Esther can handle everything for a few minutes, she thought, her eyes brimming, her energy waning. She laid her cheek on a wrinkled drawing, seeing vaguely that the office door had cracked open, but not caring.

A loud commotion in the front office roused Tillie. She had the feeling that she'd shut down her senses for a few minutes. Who was Esther arguing with?

"I'll give it to you when the boss says okay. The new boss!"

Tillie stirred, reluctant to leave her private haze. She stretched her legs under the desk. Suddenly, the restfulness of the dim, quiet office was shattered. Her eyes flew open. From beneath the kneehole in the desk came the barest of sounds. Snatches of television wildlife documentaries whipped through her mind. She felt rather than heard a motion near her ankles. She kicked both feet violently, scrambled from the desk, and screamed.

three

Footsteps sounded and the door swung wide. John Puckatt burst in with the air of a man ten years younger than his sixty-five years.

"What happened?" he yelled.

By this time, Tillie had climbed on a stool. She pointed to the desk. "Snake! There's a snake in here!"

Swiftly John grabbed a straight-backed chair and began banging it on the floor near the desk. "How big?"

"How would I know?" Tillie snapped. "It's dark under there."

"Are you sure it's a snake?" His feet skittered over the floor following the pattern of the chair legs.

"I *know* it's a snake! Believe me." She shook each foot vigorously as if to discourage the reptile joining her on the stool.

Several people gathered outside the door. Somebody flipped on the overhead lights.

Esther pushed her way through. "Get behind it, John, and chase it outside."

"How can I get behind it if I can't find it?"

"You're hemming it in. Scoot over there by Tillie and shoo it this direction," Esther ordered.

"No snake is going through that doorway with you gawkers blocking it," barked John, still scraping the chair across the floor.

"Everybody get out of the way." Esther waved her arms. "Somebody bring me the broom. Tillie, stay put."

By this time, Tillie wanted desperately to jump off the stool and join the fight but she wasn't brave enough. This female-on-a-chair-squealing-at-a-mouse image wasn't her idea of executive leadership.

"Let's toss Tillie a wastebasket," came a suggestion.

Tillie recognized Austin's voice and felt even more ridiculous.

He continued cheerfully, "When the snake shows itself, plop the basket over it."

"I've got a cheese sandwich," someone else offered. "We can use the cheese for bait to draw it out in the open where Tillie can get a good shot."

"How are you at shooting baskets, Tillie?"

Esther fired orders. "Everybody back! We're trying to chase it outside. Don't just stand there!" She aimed her ire at the owner of the cheese sandwich. "Open the outside door. Clear the way."

Feeling like a circus performer on a high wire, Tillie reached over to the top of a file cabinet and managed to pick off a drawing rolled into a tight cylinder. She poked the roll in all the crevices she could reach from her perch. To the cheers of the audience Esther hadn't been able to disperse, she stretched, jabbing the plans toward the wall behind the cabinet.

"There it is!" John yelled.

His discovery so startled Tillie that she lost her balance. The rolled-up drawing stiffened against the floor and Tillie toppled forward. A long, thin shadow shot across her path, like a fish swimming under a bridge. Falling, she tried to twist away from the shadow and landed in an awkward heap. John stood on one side of her and his chair still jabbed the floor on the other side.

The shadow stopped. A small triangular-shaped head raised itself menacingly to the level of hers. Peeking through the chair legs, Tillie faced a diamondback rattler poised to strike.

A muffled outcry rose from those watching. One of the

spectators lunged forward. Tillie cringed as Austin, wielding a length of rebar, whipped the rod through the air, deftly catching the snake and slamming it across the room. A few more blows and the snake lay motionless.

Someone helped Tillie into Wallace's chair. She drew her feet up under her. In the many years she'd been coming to Kombardee Steel—during droughts and floods, even times where nearby construction uprooted all sorts of wildlife—Tillie couldn't remember anyone encountering a rattler inside the office building. Rattlers liked their privacy. So did she.

"Think there could be two of them?" someone asked.

Esther relinquished her broom to a man to search the edges of the room.

The others, considerably sobered at finding they'd been laughing about a rattlesnake, returned to work. Esther tactfully positioned Tillie's stool to cover the spot where the snake met his demise and suggested Tillie come to the front office until someone could clean up. John Puckatt headed for the coffee machine.

Austin offered, "Don't get up. I'll push your chair and you won't have to put your feet on the floor."

She smiled weakly. "I'll be okay in a minute. How do you suppose a snake got in here?"

"This isn't a tight building. It might have strayed inside and hidden in some corner." He pointed to a small, square refrigerator on the floor near Wallace's desk. "It could have been behind there."

Tillie hadn't seen the refrigerator before. "Even so, why would a snake suddenly wander out of hiding and go exploring under my feet?"

Austin's blue eyes crinkled mischievously, but he observed calmly, "It might have been startled and gone searching for a quieter spot." Austin looked doubtfully at the narrow crevice between the door and the floor.

Tillie followed his gaze and then remembered noticing that the door had been slightly ajar before the snake made his presence known. But hadn't it been closed earlier? A weird idea entered her mind. For anyone to play that kind of sick prank was unthinkable. She blotted out the thought and unwound herself from the chair. Already on the threshold of hysterics, she remembered John Puckatt chasing the snake. A nervous giggle surfaced.

"Glad you can laugh about it." Austin studied the doorsill.

"I was picturing John doing that fancy dance routine with the chair, kind of a cross between fencing and training lions. I had no idea he was so light on his feet."

Tillie suddenly remembered Austin's part in the little drama. She paused on her way out and said, "Your golf swing has improved tremendously since the last time I saw it. Thanks."

Later, back at her familiar desk in the front office and feeling more like herself, Tillie asked Esther, "What was all the yelling about right before I started my own show?"

"I don't remember anybody yelling except you."

Tillie decided that their relationship was due for a shift in character. Esther's informality was welcome, but sometimes her tongue wagged on a fine line. That last answer had tilted toward impertinence.

She restated her question firmly. "I heard loud voices, Esther, and yours was the loudest. What happened?"

Esther said defiantly, "I thought I should handle it. That John Puckatt is no longer an employee. He came in here with a receipt for something or other and wanted money from petty cash. A lot bigger charge than Wallace ever allowed from petty cash." She pointed to a side drawer in her desk. "It would have wiped me out."

"A receipt for what?"

"Who knows what? He doesn't work here anymore. He has no right to come asking for money. If he had any due him, he should have settled before he left."

"Well, Esther, if we owe him money. . . ."

"It's your decision." The office manager straightened the collar on her blouse and studied the ceiling. "I was going to turn him over to you anyway." Her attention transferred from the ceiling to the back office. "Where did he go?"

Tillie looked out front. John's Porsche, parked two car-widths from adjacent vehicles, gleamed in the sunlight. "I'll find him."

A glance in the operations manager's office showed that it was empty. Tillie let herself out the side door and walked across the wide space between the office and the shop. A forklift operator touched his hat and brought the loaded forklift to a halt. She waved him on. Not seeing John, she walked out behind the shop.

To her left was a storage area for vehicles, loosely assembled by parking three old enclosed truck trailers on blocks to form three sides of a square. A tin roof peaking over the center gave meager protection from the elements. Skirts installed beneath the trailers helped to keep the wind at bay. The three trailers, accessible by steps to side doors, served as extra storage or even crude office space. Tillie noticed, however, that the latest occupants of the trailers had been pigeons, not ironworkers.

Today, two flatbed trucks were parked inside the enclosure, along with a gray late-model, full-size pickup.

Tillie stopped short at the sight of the Chevy pickup. A moan escaped her lips. It was Wallace's truck. Seeing it brought an onslaught of sorrow more violent than any she'd felt, even during the funeral itself. Wallace had taken such pride in that truck. He'd bought it new and, for the first time in his life, had felt financially able to order it outfitted the way he wanted, right down to its black leather seats.

She lovingly ran her fingers over the door handle, as though this lifeless piece of machinery could share her grief. *If only he'd been driving this heavy truck on Wednesday.* He had taken Dee's little car because it needed a wheel alignment. Dee had never been good with cars and earlier in the week had tangled forcefully with the curb on the way into her church's parking lot.

Tillie turned to a thirty-foot construction trailer parked across from the shed and behind the shop. Its red paint, by virtue of color, resembled rust, but the trailer was in good shape. The field men had adopted it as a combination office-lounge.

Behind the trailer an expanse of treeless, flat land made up the balance of the fenced three acres that were leased by the company. Scattered across that extra space were a weed-covered loading dock that Kombardee had never used, sprigs of obsolete railroad track, some unoperable vehicles, and a collection of discards. Tillie shaded her eyes. The dock and the track had always been there but she didn't remember so much junk.

John Puckatt bounded down the construction trailer's steps, talking over his shoulder to someone inside. At the sight of Tillie, he hurried to meet her.

"Tillie, I can't tell you how sorry I am that I wasn't here when Wallace. . . when all this happened." He took her hands in his neatly manicured ones and squeezed.

She murmured a few words meant to absolve him from guilt and wondered at the strangeness of sympathy. She expected people to offer it and she felt comforted by it, but at the same time it renewed her grief. "How's retirement?" She spoke with an effort.

"Me retired? You know better. Gotta keep the old brain spinning."

"Sure."

"Actually, that's why I was out of town this past week. Sizing up a couple of opportunities."

"Oh? You're job-hunting?"

"More along the investment line." He dropped Tillie's hands and stood back. "So, you're taking over."

His gaze put Tillie on the defensive. She'd have to get used to being judged. "That's what Uncle Wallace wanted."

"He thought the world of you. A family's a wonderful thing, for most people, that is." John and his wife had ended their marriage at least twenty years before, without children. He turned the diamond ring on his left pinky thoughtfully. He pulled his sunglasses from where they nested in his thick, wavy hair, now sprinkled liberally with gray. "Well, how did we get on that subject?"

She smiled. "I don't know. But I do want to thank you for coming to my rescue back there in the office."

"Good workout." He did a couple of quick steps and lunged with an imaginary chair. "Well, I have to get on to an appointment."

"Wait," she said. "Esther mentioned a petty cash bill."

"Not important. I was driving out here anyway and happened to find it in my pocket."

"Stop before you go and tell Esther I said to take care of it."

John shrugged. "Sure."

They walked toward the office. "We'll miss you around here," she told him.

"You'll do okay. I'll drop in. Call me if you have questions that nobody else can answer. If I'm not there, leave a message and I'll get back to you."

After lunch with a friend at the coffee shop in Malverns, Tillie made her way to the store's human resources department. Walking through the familiar aisles lined with tasteful fashions, she contrasted the morning's work environment with this up-scale store's bright lighting and artful displays.

She talked a few minutes with the director of the department. "I'm sorry not to give more notice, but I have to request a leave of absence. I'm needed to help with my family's business."

"Do you plan to return to your job here?"

Tillie smoothed the slim skirt she'd worn that day, a poor choice for one dodging snakes. Her answer came in a tremulous whisper, "Yes." She repeated with more certainty, "Yes."

Until this minute, she hadn't faced that question, although it had been in the back of her mind to resume her life after a reasonable period. She would need time to bring the business up to par. After that, she could hire a good staff for the actual operations and she would be free to ease back into her own pursuits.

She had a lot to learn about retailing, and Malverns was the perfect place to gain that experience. She relaxed, feeling the burden of her inherited responsibilities lessen slightly.

A new idea suddenly occurred to her. Sure, she could do that—oversee the business from a distance, hiring people to run it—but there was another solution that would free her from even that responsibility. Tillie could restore Kombardee Steel to its former vitality and then actively search for a buyer to purchase the company at its normal value.

Wallace loved the company, but he'd turned it over to her, trusting her to do her best to ensure Dee's future. What could be better? Tillie would sell and carefully invest the proceeds to provide Dee with a stream of cash for the rest of her life. She'd employ a financial planner for investment advice.

The insistent drumming of fingertips on the desk in front of her snapped Tillie's thoughts back to the situation at hand. She apologized for her lapse of attention and quickly accepted the form the personnel director offered.

Before leaving the store, Tillie bought two tailored, blue chambray dresses with shirt-type tops and full skirts. She paired them with low-heeled pumps, leather belts, and colorful jewelry. She wanted to look like the boss but yet be able to interact daily with shop and field workers.

Parking her car back at the plant, Tillie's mind switched to that morning when she'd arrived in time to see a potential customer leave in a huff because he couldn't find what he wanted to buy. She wished she'd remembered to ask John Puckatt why inventory was so low.

She decided to get a handle on the money situation. Payroll was first. Kombardee Steel employed an accounting firm, Blackbourn Accountants, to do payroll and also audit the books, make tax returns, and be on call for consulting. As far as Tillie could tell, Esther had supplied payroll data to the accountants when she was supposed to. Employees had been receiving their checks on time. Tillie would have heard if they hadn't.

Between interruptions, Tillie worked at the computer most of the afternoon. Esther answered what questions she could.

"Who is Lynn Lippincott?" Tillie wondered when she came across a typed memo with a payroll summary.

"New accountant, from the same firm. Comes in a lot more than any of the others ever did. Are you going to keep that same outfit?" Esther sounded hopeful for a negative answer.

"For now. Why?"

"Well, I think it's confusing. They pay some of the bills and Wallace was paying the rest."

Tillie thought the accounting firm made out only payroll checks for the field and shop. Everything else was paid by checks handwritten from a company checkbook that her uncle kept in his office. Accounts payable had not been computerized. She'd often signed the company checks herself, including payroll for the office and management.

"What kind of bills do they pay?"

"I'm not privy to such information, but I guess they've been paying almost everything that Wallace hasn't."

"Almost everything?"

Esther suddenly found it necessary to clean between the buttons on her phone with a tissue. Her answer was more of a complaint than an accusation. "Seems that a lot more overdue notices come across my desk than should."

"What kind of things?"

"Oh, bills. Maybe some are personal. I don't know."

"Well, Esther, are the vendors getting paid?"

"As far as I know."

"Then what are you talking about?"

"More odds and ends. Insurance maybe, things like that." Esther shut off her information pipeline. "I have to take this out to the shop. Can you catch the phones?"

Accounts receivable was on the computer and seemed to be down. Alarmed, when Esther returned Tillie asked, "Is the billing up to date?"

"As much as it can be, considering all the rush stuff that I have to do first."

Tillie picked up the phone, "I'm calling Janice. You need help." She couldn't expect money in the bank if the office didn't bill jobs on time.

There was no answer at Janice's number.

"Out shopping," Esther guessed.

"Or in the hospital. She did call in sick, you know."

"More likely shopping."

"I'll try her later. But we need somebody for the other desk anyway."

Tillie made another call and arranged for a temp to be there the next morning. She turned her attention back to the books.

The last two company bank statements were still sealed in their mailing envelopes. Tillie tore one open, preparing to balance it. She studied the first check with concern. The information entered had been typed. The scrawled signature in heavy, black pen hardly looked like Wallace's. His penmanship had never been neat but this was barely legible. Others bore a similar irregular signature, and she'd signed a few herself. However, as Tillie flipped through the canceled checks, she was shocked to discover a new signature. Signed with a flourish, employing a distinctive jag where others might embellish with a curl, was the name, *Lynn Lippincott*.

Rapidly she compared the canceled checks with the statement and then with accounts payable. Everything seemed in order, even though the ending balance was a little low.

You're being possessive, she chastised herself. But she decided to ask Dee why Wallace had felt it necessary to give an outsider such privileges.

Another attempt at Janice's number was fruitless. Tillie copied it in her address book to try again that night.

Shortly before closing time, Tillie went back to Wallace's office. There was no sign of the dead rattler or a live companion, but to be safe, she clacked her heels noisily across the floor to the desk. She sighed. The task ahead seemed hopeless. She pushed aside loose papers and thin folders and deliberately chose a thick folder. She sat down, opened it, and went to work sorting its contents.

She was pleasantly surprised to find some order to the stack. Much of it was invoices or notices of payments due. Curiously, some of the bills were late. That was uncharacteristic of Wallace. He had always kept a close eye on cash flow, and the company's credit rating never faltered.

Tillie came to a statement for a life insurance premium. She retraced her way back through the papers, recalling another from that same company. She found a third buried near the bottom. Esther's hint had been prophetic. The premium was long overdue. Perhaps Wallace had dropped that policy or these were duplicates of a premium statement already paid.

Esther appeared at the door. "I'm leaving in fifteen minutes. Have to get out of here on time tonight."

"Thanks, Esther."

The office manager propped her hands on her hips. "It's my nail night."

"That's fine. Leave whenever you're ready." Tillie continued putting the bills in order.

"I'm waiting on you."

Impatiently, Tillie assured Esther, "Don't wait. I want to work a while."

"There won't be another person here after I leave."

Touched by the note of concern from this woman who had served her uncle faithfully for ten years, Tillie said, "Sit down a moment, please. Let's talk."

Esther settled herself stiffly, fingering the dark red ringlets dangling in front of her earlobes.

Tillie noticed tired lines in the woman's full face. For all Esther's blustery energy, she had a heart irregularity. Tillie told her, "My uncle always appreciated everything you did for him. Dee, too."

The corners of Esther's generous mouth tilted upward slightly. "Well, I'll admit, he was kind of a grouch lately, and getting more so. Don't know why. Kind of secretive, too, you know." Esther hastened to diffuse the barb. "Now, don't get me wrong. He was a fine man."

"I hope you'll stay on with me, Esther. I really need you."

Esther was obviously pleased. "I'll stay." She quickly followed up with a shake of her finger. "Provided I get some reliable help."

"I promise we'll ease your workload right away," Tillie assured her. "All companies have problems. We may have more than our share, but nothing that can't be solved. Did my uncle talk to you about anyone he had in mind to replace John Puckatt?"

Esther lowered her eyes and shook her head firmly, the ringlets swinging with her emphatic reply. Esther's antagonism toward John Puckatt was never far from the surface.

"We need a new operations manager right away." Considering Esther's built-in aversion to the last person in that position, she cautioned, "We need someone strong in that job." Tillie hoped Esther could avoid clashing with the new one. For a second, Tillie wondered about the sparks between the office manager and the operations manager. Both were unmarried and with John's youthful demeanor, the age difference was tolerable. Could it be? Esther and John Puckatt?

Tillie took another look at Esther. Aloud, she ticked off tasks ahead for the office staff, ending with a list meant more for herself. "We have a start on the accounts. I'll need to give a pep talk to everyone. Haven't written any letters yet. Did you get the news release out to *The County Daily?*"

"I'll drop it by the post office after I get my nails done. They wanted me to fax it over, but I said we didn't have one."

The thought of shopping for office equipment plummeted to the bottom of Tillie's list as she remembered something else. A day had gone by and she hadn't even checked to see how many workers were in the field on how many jobs. Yes, she needed an operations manager badly. "Go close up, Esther. You'll be late for your nails. I'll be ready when you are."

Before Tillie locked Wallace's office, she made a note to ask Austin to help her review the bidding on new jobs. She also called Blackbourn Accountants and arranged for Lynn Lippincott to come to the office the next day. If Ms. Lippincott were authorized to sign checks on Tillie's company, she wanted to get acquainted with her.

Esther was already sitting in her blue Buick when Tillie reached the front office door. Robert Sandoval, the shop foreman, fidgeted near the gate, tossing a rock into the air, catching it the first time and missing it the next. *How thoughtful of him to wait*, she thought. Tillie would make sure she had the right keys so she could come and go independently.

The phone rang. She almost ignored it, but picked it up with a quick hello, forgetting to answer with the company name.

"Tillie?" Dee's soft voice sounded agitated. "Can you drive over to the house on your way home?"

"Sure, I was going to call you later."

"Don't wait. Come over right now. I think something awful has happened."

"What's the matter? Are you sick?"

"No, but I'm in trouble, Tillie. You'd better come now."

four

Dee had been watching out a window for Tillie. She jerked the front door open before her niece could knock.

"Thank goodness you're here." The older woman burst into tears. Although her aunt was two inches taller than she, Tillie gathered Dee into her arms. "What happened?" she asked. "Tell me what's wrong."

Dee dropped to the living room couch as if all strength had deserted her.

"Please, Aunt Dee, don't cry. Should I call the doctor?"

Dee shook her head. Tillie wanted to call somebody. She needed help handling a problem of the magnitude that would send Dee into such fits of sobbing. "Where's Austin?"

"Oh, oh. . . ," Dee moaned, rubbing her fingers nervously over the floral fabric on the couch cushion. "I'm not sure what will become of me."

"What are you talking about?"

Dee fluttered her hand toward the coffee table where a thick, folded document protruded from a plastic envelope. "Look at it. I called the insurance company."

Tillie hurriedly freed the sheets of paper from the plastic envelope and smoothed the stubborn folds flat. She saw at once that the document was an insurance policy on Wallace's life with Dee as beneficiary. It listed a sizeable face value.

"Don't feel badly, Aunt Dee. Uncle Wallace meant for you to have the money. He took out the policy so you'd have a nest egg to live on when. . . when anything happened to him."

"I would feel bad enough if there were money. But there's

not, and I still feel terrible."

"I don't understand."

Dee burst into fresh sobs. "The policy is worthless."

"Impossible!" Tillie scanned the pages. The term insurance was written by a sound, well-known company, taken out right after Wallace and Dee had married. "I'll call the agent tomorrow." She suddenly remembered the past-due notice she'd seen at the office and her voice lost a degree of confidence. "You don't have to do a thing." She hoped feverishly that the notice did not concern this particular policy.

"That's a problem too. We don't have our old agent, the one listed on that envelope. He died last year himself." She looked incredulous, as if the man had broken some unwritten rule that life insurance agents must outlive their clients. "Now we've got this new one and Wallace despised him."

"Oh, come on," Tillie countered gently. "I don't remember Uncle Wallace despising people."

"Well, he did this man. They argued a lot over the phone, just a couple of weeks ago."

"What about?"

"Wallace said they couldn't keep their records straight. He told me the insurance agent had called him a liar."

"So the company is withholding payment?"

Dee shook her head violently. "More than that. They say the policy is no good. They say Wallace didn't make premium payments and that it's way past the grace period."

"You mean, they're threatening not to pay anything on this policy?" The premium notices in Wallace's office loomed menacingly in Tillie's mind. "We'll see about that." She refused to believe the worst had happened, that the company had legitimately canceled the policy. Her uncle would never have carelessly neglected to pay premiums, unless . . . . A new thought hit her. "Maybe Uncle Wallace let this policy lapse on purpose. Maybe he had taken out a better one."

Dee brightened at the suggestion. "He did apply to another company. Several, I think. But," she said disconsolately as her shoulders slumped, "I don't believe we got a new policy."

"Now, don't worry. I'm sure if Uncle Wallace did intend to drop this, he would have first arranged for another to take its place."

Dee wasn't consoled. "I think that medical man caused trouble." She lowered her voice secretively. "You know, Wallace was borderline diabetic."

Tillie was aware of her uncle's tendency toward diabetes, although he passed it off as unimportant. "But would a borderline diabetic, one not requiring medication, be denied insurance? Surely your doctor could have certified that Wallace didn't have a serious health problem."

"I don't know whether or not it ever got to the point of being denied. Wallace stopped going to our doctor not long ago. Found the new one. Doesn't matter. Insurance companies have their own tests and all."

"Let me take care of it, Aunt Dee. I'll get the straight story."

Dee sat back now and smoothed her skirt. "I wonder if Wallace antagonized the other insurance agents too. You know, he was so touchy lately. Not with me, you understand," she said loyally.

"Of course not. Nor with me." Again Tillie bemoaned the fact that she hadn't actually seen Wallace for more than a month before he died.

"His behavior had changed a bit. I have to admit that. He wasn't like his old self. I don't think things were going well at work."

Tillie cringed. She could testify to that.

"You know how he always had something good to say about everyone? Well, not lately. No matter what name came up in our conversation, he made a derogatory remark about that person. He seemed distrustful of people, and worse, he seemed almost distrustful of himself. There was a sort of hesitancy, almost a fearfulness so unlike Wallace."

"I wish you'd told me."

"I couldn't put my finger on a specific problem or I would have. Goodness knows, you were good to call us so often. Wallace never wanted me to bother you with anything that wasn't necessary. He knew how important your own work was to you—getting that experience so you can open your 'frilly shop.' "

Tillie probed gently, hoping to find some clue to the general mess at work and the fact that Kombardee Steel appeared to be running in low gear. "Did Wallace talk much about any difficulties, say, equipment breaking down or the company being underbid on jobs?"

"Only general comments, but I got wind of a few things."

"Like what?"

"The work wasn't getting done, in the office or out in the field. Sloppy employees, he'd tell me. Even Esther Vargas got on his nerves."

The part about Esther didn't surprise Tillie. "By the way," she asked casually, "does the name Lynn Lippincott mean anything to you?"

Dee thought a while and then shook her head.

Tillie phrased the next question carefully. "Do you know if Uncle Wallace had given special responsibilities to anyone?"

Dee looked puzzled.

"Like authorizing other people to sign company checks?"

"Goodness, no. He would never have done that." She ticked

off on her fingers. "Only you, Wallace, and I signed checks."

Tillie decided not to alarm Dee by mentioning Lynn Lippincott's signature. "What about money? Did there seem to be a cash flow problem? I mean, was Wallace worried over paying the bills?"

Dee drew back aghast. "Wallace always paid his bills on time. There was always money in my household account."

Dee's indignation brought a welcome chuckle to Tillie's lips. Enough of this serious talk. Dee needed a change of pace, and Tillie had butted her head against enough problems for one day. She jotted down the insurance policy data and the company's phone number, then stretched, kicking off her shoes and rubbing her tired arches across the coffee table legs. "I see your pink azaleas are loaded with blossoms."

But Dee was lost in thought, her brows furrowed deeply. "I was beginning to worry a little about Wallace. He was so intense, and yet. . . ."

Obviously Dee still needed to talk. Tillie responded, "Yet?"

Dee leaned confidentially toward Tillie. "It hurts me to say this, but I can tell you, Tillie. I actually had begun to have some slight misgivings—not any real doubts, you understand, just fleeting thoughts—about Wallace's ability to run the business." She squirmed, clasping her hands until the knuckles whitened.

That assessment didn't overly alarm Tillie because Dee was the last person to judge anyone's ability to run a business.

Dee struggled on. "Some of the stories he related sounded kind of farfetched, and sometimes it almost seemed that Wallace reacted a tiny bit irrationally."

For Dee to suggest that Wallace acted irrationally was so shocking that it might carry a kernel of truth.

"Of course," Dee continued, "Wallace could never be irrational. That's what I told Austin when I wrote him."

"You wrote Austin about company problems?" Tillie sat erect, jolted by a sudden feeling of resentment.

Dee hurried to explain. "I didn't actually tell Austin to come. I never dreamed he would."

But like a good son—one who had practically disappeared for years—Austin had come running home to help out. Tillie couldn't avoid the sarcasm that colored her thoughts as she pictured the more likely scenario that he'd hurried to California to protect his mother's financial interests. She remembered a conversation with Austin that eventful summer. Austin had intimated that his mother had sunk a lot of money in Wallace's business and he was trusting that it wouldn't "disappear."

"Nice of him to come," Tillie managed.

Dee looked at her thoughtfully. "He has changed, Tillie. I know you and he had your differences that summer." She picked up a cut glass candy dish from the coffee table and traced the grooves in its pattern with her fingers. "Wallace and I had hoped that you and Austin. . . it would have been perfect, too good to be true, that the two people we loved so much. . . ."

Tillie doubted that Wallace exactly loved Austin. Austin was more of a thorn in his side, not living up to Wallace's concerted efforts to make an ironworker of him.

"Of course," Dee said as she put the candy dish down, a little of her customary twinkle returning, "now Austin is a Christian. He told me so."

This news both astounded and sent a surge of joy through Tillie. But she refused to consider the ramifications of it as far as she was concerned. "That's wonderful," she said.

Dee lapsed back into a mournful state of anxiety. "What if I don't have enough income to live?"

"Don't even think of such a thing. The house is paid for, and Kombardee Steel will provide you with a regular income."

Even after I sell the company, she added silently. "I'll come over soon and we'll spend some time taking inventory of your financial situation. You'll feel better."

Dee flung an arm the direction of the den. "Wallace didn't want me to be one of those wives who can't handle money. He tried, God bless him. He went over and over our personal records with me. They're all in there somewhere. But I'm afraid I don't understand everything." Dee dismissed the financial discussion with a glance at her watch. "You must be hungry. Come in the kitchen and have a bite to eat with me."

Tillie couldn't resist the pleading note as Dee murmured, "There's so much food out there. I'll never eat it all. People were so kind."

Tillie did what she could to help with the meal, carefully folding colorful cloth napkins in a manner that would meet with Dee's approval. Then she sat at the table by the large window that overlooked the generous backyard, a combination small, well-kept lawn and large orchard. Dee bustled between the refrigerator and cabinets and finally delivered two plates on the quilted mats, nudging a stray fork back into line.

Tillie was glad that Dee asked the blessing because it was Tillie's turn to feel teary. Sitting here in this homey kitchen brought a flood of memories. She'd lived in this house with Wallace and Dee off and on for eight years. Although she spent time away at college and now was happy in her apartment, this place would always be home to her, even more so than the house she'd shared with her parents.

The luxuriant green leaves on the fruit trees that Wallace had tenderly planted and cared for grew dark as night closed in. The guest house, where Austin stayed, was barely visible at the back of the lot. It looked deserted.

Tillie knew the quiet visit brought a satisfying comfort to Dee. Their conversation ebbed and flowed, pausing occasionally for private reminiscing until the telephone's loud ringing jarred the peaceful interlude.

Dee reached to answer it. Tillie carried the empty plates to the sink. She would put them in the dishwasher and be on her way. This had been a long, tiring day.

She closed the dishwasher door, realizing that beyond Dee's initial hello, there had been only silence. Tillie looked curiously at her aunt and saw with alarm that Dee's face had paled and she was holding the receiver out to Tillie.

"It's a police officer. Someone called them about trouble at the plant."

Tillie wiped her hands and took over. "May I help you? I'm Tillie Gibson, Mrs. Kombardy's niece."

"This is the Citrus County sheriff's office. A patrol car is out at Kombardee Steel. We're trying to contact whoever is responsible for the premises."

Conscious of her aunt's feelings, Tillie turned to the wall and spoke quietly into the mouthpiece. "I'm that person. Is there a problem out there?"

"A neighbor reported some unusual activity. We checked it out. You may have had a break-in."

After Tillie listened anxiously to the meager details, she hung up and explained the situation to Dee. As she did so, the back door opened and Austin walked in.

Dee whirled toward him and exclaimed, "Austin, I didn't think you were home. There's trouble at the plant."

"I'm going out there," Tillie said, heading for the living room and scooping up her purse. "The police are waiting."

Austin overtook her. "Come on. I'll drive."

Dee followed them outside and stood by Austin's Explorer.

"Call me as soon as you can."

Austin drove a shade too recklessly for Tillie's taste but it was a controlled recklessness. She pictured him bumping over rough, rural roads, a geologist at work.

The two police officers were polite and efficient. They inquired about people who would have access to the property.

Embarrassed, Tillie named those she knew. "There's the office manager, Esther Vargas, and the shop foreman, Robert Sandoval." Dismayed, she realized that she hadn't the least idea who else might have keys, or who had keys to the gates.

She put in a call to the shop foreman on the slim chance that he might have come there that evening. His wife said that he'd gone for a few things at the market and, no, he hadn't said anything about going to Kombardee. Esther Vargas didn't answer her phone, but she would never come to the office at night.

The officers found no signs of forced entry into the main building. They asked Tillie if anything appeared to be missing.

Even though she'd worked there at widely spaced intervals of late, Tillie felt she'd know if anything obvious had been stolen. She made a perfunctory check and then shrugged her shoulders.

Austin strode in from the yard. "The big equipment and the trucks are still here. A few things that would be easy to cart off are here—like an air compressor and some small tools that were left out. Who reported the problem?"

"Your neighbor." The officer pointed in the direction of a manufacturing business beyond the chain-link fence. The company made replacement parts for heavy equipment. "The owner happened to come out to pick up something he needed from his office. Got suspicious that anybody should be here, maybe because of the death and all." The officer looked away from

Tillie momentarily. "He thought he saw car lights leaving as he was calling. Couldn't identify the vehicle. When we arrived, the wide gate was standing open."

Tillie looked puzzled. "The foreman closed the small one after I pulled out. I saw him in my rear-view mirror, and the other was already closed." She offered, "Perhaps the lock wasn't fastened properly or someone was able to pick it. Let's hope that it was simply a matter of someone stealing a few reinforcing rods, and whoever it was won't be back."

The officers showed signs of departing. Tillie thanked them and asked Austin if he minded staying for a few minutes.

While he checked the other doors to the building, which had already been checked by the officers, Tillie went into Wallace's office. Remembering the snake episode, she made plenty of noise. Somewhere Wallace kept a key register and spare keys.

She gingerly removed the framed landscape from the wall and swung open the door of the unlocked safe. Shoved to the back was the register, a thick book-type container, its interior fitted with fasteners, some empty and some holding keys. The accompanying chart listed names of people who had checked out keys.

Tillie found her own name; Esther, John Puckatt, and Robert Sandoval had office keys and gate keys as well. Obviously, the register was not up to date. John would have turned in his keys upon resignation. Austin's name didn't even appear, and Tillie knew other keys had been issued and returned since the last entry in the register. She sighed. One more task to take care of.

She replaced the key register and closed the safe, carefully rehanging the landscape. Even in this stressful moment, the familiar scene provided a respite. The painting of the high mountain range had been done during one of southern California's brief winter seasons. Puffy clouds hovered in a cerulean blue sky. Brilliant white snow capped the upper reaches of the mountains, emphasizing their towering heights and creating a sight to rival the Alps.

As she turned from the painting, she remembered she had left Wallace's ledger in the lower drawer of his desk that afternoon. The ledger probably should be stored in the safe. She bent down, opened the drawer, and pulled out the heavy book. To her surprise, several white legal-sized envelopes toppled over, falling into its place. They must have been standing on edge in the drawer behind the ledger. She did not remember seeing any envelopes when she'd put away the ledger earlier.

She sat down and studied the open drawer. The four plain white envelopes were stamped and sealed, as if ready to be mailed. They had been roughly addressed in heavy black pen by someone with almost illegible handwriting. Before Austin poked his head in the door, she wasn't even able to decipher the addressee on the top one.

"Everything okay here?"

She shoved the ledger toward Austin. "Maybe this should go in the safe."

He turned and deftly picked the landscape off the office wall, opened the safe, and inserted the ledger.

Tillie kept her eyes on Austin. He would know about the unlocked safe. Probably everyone in the office did. Maybe the shop people too. She reached for the envelopes and slipped them into her purse. She stood up, shutting the drawer with her leg. "I'm ready."

"I heard what you told the police about this break-in hopefully being a one-time occurrence."

"I'm not too worried," Tillie said confidently. "There are a lot of small-time operators in the construction business. I've been around long enough to know that some can't or won't pay their bills."

"So you're willing to accept the theory that somebody needed a few bars of iron for a patio job and decided to steal them?"

"I don't like to be cheated, but yes." She stopped at Esther's desk. "I forgot to call Aunt Dee. She'll be worried."

While she made the call, Austin paced and then said decisively, "We need more security around here. Something worse could happen."

They left by the front door. She jiggled the door handle vigorously. "You'd think that floodlights and locks and a tall fence would be enough."

Austin dismissed with a wave of his hand the floods that illuminated the grounds and the doorways. "Obviously, they aren't, at least in this isolated area."

"Okay, okay," she said irritably. "I'll see about it."

He opened her side first. "You've got enough to do. I'll take care of it."

His high-handed manner didn't sit well with Tillie. She balanced herself, one foot inside the vehicle, and told him, "Yes, that will be fine." Secretly, it was a relief to have even one chore erased from her to do list, but she didn't like Austin making executive decisions for her.

She was silent on the ride back to Dee's. Her hands clutched her purse as she wondered about the white envelopes. The scribbling on them appeared to match the heavy, jagged scrawl of Wallace's before he died. Obviously he'd written letters that had never been mailed, but she would wait until she was alone to examine them.

five

Arriving at her apartment, Tillie reached to the visor and pushed the button on the garage door opener. The door creaked up and she pulled into the double garage. She carefully guided the car into the single space left between the rows of neatly categorized bins on metal shelving and numerous sturdy boxes. She was particularly cautious of a bulky unopened crate that housed a glass-fronted curio cabinet. When friends asked how she could have accumulated so much, she explained she was a collector of merchandise and ideas, all part of her plan to establish her own retail shop.

Her entire apartment was an eclectic mixture of old and new. A few antique furniture pieces were interspersed with more traditional items. Like most rentals, her apartment had off-white walls and neutral carpeting. This bland background formed the perfect shell for whatever arrangements she fancied. Incorporating exquisite samples of lace and linens, along with some fine ceramic work and framed prints, into her decor served as a trial run for displaying merchandise.

The living room on the first floor of the townhouse was small, as were the dining area, kitchen, and guest bath. A patio outside the dining area stretched the usable space. Upstairs, the bath and two bedrooms were roomy. One bedroom served as her office, complete with file cabinet and desk.

A light rain began to fall as she brought in her mail. Rain was an oddity, even in the winter season, always creating an undercurrent of excitement for Tillie. She poured a glass of milk and curled up on the sofa, a well-worn gold frieze relic from her parents' house that she ached to discard. Someday she'd find the right one to replace it at the same time she had money to spend.

She eagerly opened a letter from her parents and read it twice while she finished the milk, feeling a pang of loneliness mixed with a bit of self-pity for being apart from them at such a tremulous time.

Next, she reached into her purse for the white envelopes taken from Wallace's bottom desk drawer. Examining the uneven black scrawl on the envelopes, she saw that in the upper left corner was the Kombardy home address. Each one was addressed to the insurance company that issued the policy Dee had shown her a few hours before.

Tillie gingerly opened one, feeling all the while as if she were committing a federal offense. She pulled out two pieces of paper. The first was a premium notice. The second was a check made out to the insurance company, dated months before and signed by Wallace. The check was written on a personal account that Wallace kept separate from Dee's household money and from the company account. She recalled that he rarely used that account. The checkbook and statements were probably somewhere in his belongings at work, waiting for her attention.

She could only wonder what might have happened to the preaddressed printed envelope that ordinarily accompanied premium notices. Yes, Wallace's writing left a lot to be desired, but these envelopes certainly were legible enough to have been read and delivered. The checks could have been cashed. . . if they had been put in the mail.

An agonizing pressure gripped Tillie's chest and refused to go away. She was sure that tomorrow's call to the insurance company would confirm what Dee had been told and what these checks bore out: The premium payments on Wallace's insurance policy had not been received and credited.

But why? Tillie wrestled with that question as she turned out the lights and climbed the stairs. She wanted to believe that Wallace had, for reasons of his own, held back on mailing the payments. Had those envelopes been slipped in the desk drawer only that day?

She stepped into the shower and tilted her face up to the soothing spray of water. Wallace wasn't here to explain why the policy had lapsed, or, for that matter, why about anything. Tillie flicked off the water and groped for a towel. As she dried her face, rivulets of tears ran down her cheeks. She made little effort to stem their flow.

Tillie crawled into the cool sheets and shivered, mentally evaluating the several Kombardee employees who could have paid a visit to Wallace's desk after she'd put the ledger away. No wonder that, as Dee said, Wallace had shown signs of distrusting people around him. Tillie was rapidly becoming distrustful too.

Through the night it rained and the sky was still overcast the next morning when Tillie entered the office.

She eyed Janice's desk hopefully. No luck. But at the other desk sat a young woman who appeared to be in her late teens. She was attractive with rather long dark brown hair. Blue eyes shone from behind owlish glasses with an appealing clarity, and her fingers flew across the keyboard.

Encouraged, Tillie looked to Esther for an introduction.

"This is Janelle from the temp agency," Esther said, and offered a rare compliment. "She was here bright and early." Esther's index finger drew an arc between the empty desk and the one where Janelle paused in her typing. "First Janice, now Janelle. It's confusing."

No sooner had Esther articulated the problem than she provided the solution by marching to Janice's desk. She swooped up the nameplate and slapped a length of masking tape over the last three letters of Janice's name and promptly repositioned it in front of Janelle. Tillie guessed that was the end of Janice, and Janelle now had a nickname.

Tillie asked Esther to come into Wallace's office. "I want a short staff meeting. Two o'clock this afternoon." At Esther's blank look, she explained, "Everyone in this building plus the shop foreman. No one from the field."

Esther nodded. Tillie handed her a tablet. Esther took her cue, pulled a pencil from the ringlets, and wrote something on the pad.

Tillie discussed office procedures, in particular the processing of mail. "I'd like you to handle the incoming mail personally." She watched Esther's expression carefully at the mention of mail. There were no startling revelations. "All outgoing mail is to be put in a basket on your desk. I want you to see that anything deposited there after the mail carrier's pickup goes directly to the post office with you or me. Or Austin can take it. If that's not possible, put it in your file cabinet overnight. And Esther, from now on, we'll keep your file cabinet locked."

If Esther questioned the procedures, she didn't do so aloud, merely adding, "I already lock my desk. That's where the petty cash is."

"Good. I need a computer terminal back in my office. See if you can get somebody to bring that one from my old desk in here and set it up."

"Austin is good with computers."

That was a new facet of Austin's talents.

At the end of the session, Tillie said, "One more thing, Esther. Could you please take the wreath off the front door?" The crack in her voice was barely detectable. Esther gave her approval with another note, heartily underlined.

Tillie's call to the insurance company regarding Wallace's policy was, as she feared, useless. She would talk to Ralph Delanoy about it when he returned, but she doubted that he could do anything.

Fifteen minutes before Lynn Lippincott of the accounting firm was to arrive, Tillie had partially cleared Wallace's desk and was ready for the meeting. She had been able to locate little in the way of records or paperwork to show what Blackbourn Accountants had been doing.

Esther buzzed her. "Blackbourn called. Lippincott will be late."

Irritated, Tillie went on to something else. Later, a sharp rap at the door so startled her that she toppled a pencil holder. Wallace had bought the redwood holder, shaped like a hollow tree trunk, on a trip to Redwood National Park. She scrambled awkwardly to scoop up the pencils, calling, "Come in."

Tillie stared in confusion at the dark-haired woman who breezed through the door wearing a charcoal-black suit with a red silk blouse. Her outfit would have taken the prize in a power-dressing contest.

"I'm Lynn Lippincott from Blackbourn Accountants." Without waiting to be invited, the woman sat in the visitor's chair opposite Tillie and put her black leather briefcase on a nearby table.

Tillie stalled, precisely arranging the pencils in the redwood trunk. After gathering her wits, she still felt at a disadvantage, a feeling that showed no signs of evaporating when Ms. Lippincott extracted a notebook computer from her briefcase. Tillie marveled at the contrast in their appearance. The blue chambray dress Tillie wore was hardly adequate. She should have worn something stronger. . . like a crown.

Tillie's efforts to lead the discussion succeeded, on the surface. But soon she realized that Lynn Lippincott had assumed the role of instructor, methodically explaining to Tillie the reports her firm generated. Instead of Tillie outlining what Kombardee Steel needed, the CPA was telling her how Kombardee Steel could operate under the system Blackbourn Accounts had put in place.

Soon Tillie stopped sputtering, "But, what if. . . ." and began to absorb as much as she could. When the hour-long meeting was nearly over, her nerves were shot. Finally, as if she had been in control all along, Tillie directed, "I want to receive regular copies of every report, entry, and statement. Anything that you or your firm generates in connection with my business." Her lower lip seemed to quiver after such a bold statement.

Ms. Lippincott said smoothly, "Of course," shut down her computer, and closed her briefcase.

But Tillie had a more sensitive matter to settle. "Your firm was hired to do our payroll. You issue the weekly paychecks for our field and other hourly employees."

"Yes?"

"But I noticed your signature on checks written on our company account. Can you tell me why?"

Lynn Lippincott's complexion faded briefly to match the hue of premature gray that streaked from her forehead back through her black hair like a swath of misplaced makeup. "It was your uncle's idea. He felt, shall we say, slightly overwhelmed at handling all the details of running this office. You can see that the business has dipped slightly into the negative. Any measure to relieve the paperwork seemed a logical way to allow Mr. Kombardy to use his time and energies in a more hands-on manner."

Dipping slightly into the negative politely but grossly understated their recent performance. To Tillie, the business was gathering speed on a downhill slide.

Ms. Lippincott continued. "You understand, the scope of our services to this company had expanded from simple payroll accounting. As our responsibilities increased, it became necessary for me to spend more time on the premises and involve myself with a wider range of tasks."

Tillie made a mental note to verify with Esther the frequency of Ms. Lippincott's visits to this office. Then she crossed out that note, telling herself she was acting paranoid.

Outside the rain resumed, now pelting against the window. Nothing would get done in the field today.

"Of course," the CPA suggested, "if you plan to work here full time, you may want to sign most of the checks yourself."

Tillie moved forward in Wallace's big leather chair, put her elbows on the desk, and made herself as tall as possible. This woman could probably recite the tax tables forward and backward. "I not only plan to work here, Ms. Lippincott, I intend to operate the company. My signature will be required on every check except those generated by your payroll service. I thank you for making yourself so available to my uncle." But she decided to take one further step toward reversing the tail-wagging-the-dog situation. "I will retain Blackbourn Accountants for the present. If possible, I would like you to continue as our auditor as well as provide the payroll service. To help in making long-range plans, however, it would be a good idea if you submitted a written proposal outlining your services."

Ms. Lippincott's lips smiled sweetly, although the rest of her anatomy remained rigid. "I'll ask one of the secretaries in the office to send over something."

"Fine."

When she left, Tillie closed the door and then raised both fists in the air. "I can fire her! Yes, I can!" she mouthed so softly it couldn't be heard outside the room.

Tillie plopped down in Wallace's chair and closed her eyes. Her head hurt with a fury. She didn't intend to get rid of Blackbourn Accountants, or Lynn Lippincott. That was one smart woman, and Tillie could use smart advice.

She worked until noon drawing up a calendar for bookkeeping jobs to be done in their office and noted the days when financial reports were due from Blackbourn. She resolved to make sure from now on that she got a complete accounting of everything that firm did for Kombardee.

She smiled. Kombardee Steel felt like her company, even if it were a temporary arrangement. Wallace would like that.

The detailers and estimators from the back rooms migrated to the main office about two o'clock for the staff meeting. To Tillie, some looked like they were attending their second funeral within a week. She felt fairly confident as she perched on the corner of the front desk opposite Esther's, adopting what she hoped was a friendly stance. She told herself that these people needed reassurance that the company and their jobs were stable, and she meant to give it to them.

Esther circulated a copy of the press release regarding Wallace's death and Tillie's assumption of his duties. She directed everyone to an open photograph album she had put out on Janice's empty desk. In it were pictures that showed various stages of a job done the year before, an underground parking structure for a small apartment building.

Tillie recognized one or two of the Kombardee ironworkers with tool belts and hard hats placing the steel. One shot was a close-up of bundles of reinforcing rods. Kombardee did both the placing and fabricating of the steel, so she knew the bundles of steel in the photograph had been cut to size and bent on the bending machine to the proper angle back in their shop. The bundles had been tagged and delivered to the job on a company flatbed truck. Tillie squinted at the image of a man who stood off to one side consulting plans.

Austin came and looked over her shoulder.

"I remember that man." She pointed to the photograph. "He was a field foreman. Worked here for as long as I can remember." She tapped her forehead. "Oh, what was his name?"

"Earl Jessup," answered Austin.

"That's it. When I first began to tag along with Uncle Wallace to job sites, that man would joke with me about being too young to get in the union. He'd take my hands and lift me over the ditches I couldn't jump."

"A prince of a man."

Austin's remark rang strangely hollow, but Tillie agreed, "Yes, he was." She turned the page. "How did you happen to remember his name?"

"There are few secrets in this business." Austin moved to join the other employees.

Tillie didn't understand his choice of words, but she was busy choosing her own as she opened the informal meeting.

A strange quiet settled over the group, interrupted by a phone call that Janelle answered and handled with a series of short murmurs.

Esther, pencil and pad poised, said, "Where is that Sandy?"

Just then Robert Sandoval, dark-haired and swarthy, hurriedly made his appearance. The shop foreman spied a seat several steps away and, in getting there, brushed violently against a four-drawer file cabinet. The compactly built thirty-nine year old was known for strength that matched the iron bending machine under his supervision, and clumsiness. The two attributes balanced each other nicely, and he'd yet to come in to the office to fill out an accident report for himself.

A bright sun shone now, glimmering on the still wet cars out front and streaming in the front windows. Somehow facing everyone seemed less forbidding against a backdrop of cheery sunlight, Tillie surmised.

Tillie thanked everyone for their personal concerns, for their loyalty to Wallace, and generally tried to convince them that the company would continue operating and their jobs were secure. She thought she'd done a fair job when she proceeded to a pep talk on the necessity of everyone performing in tip-top form. She had just made the point that the health of the company depended on quality work from its employees when she was interrupted by the side door cracking open.

A hoarse whisper summoned Sandoval, who clumped over to the door. He held a short conversation with a red-faced shop worker.

Tillie gathered from the man's colorful description of a forklift that it had ceased operation.

Sandoval turned apologetically to Tillie. "We've got to move that steel and the forklift's broke again."

"Go, take care of it," she excused him.

"That no-good hunk of junk never was any good, and the good one's broke permanentlike."

When the two finally let themselves out and shut the door, Tillie tried to make the best of the interruption. "As I was saying, quality workmanship is what we need," she laughed feebly, "accomplished with quality tools."

About that time, Sandoval poked his head back inside. "I'll be back as soon as I get that. . . er. . . er, that old forklift fixed."

His attempt to curb his language evoked some snickers. He grinned knowingly and left, slamming the door with a gusto that rattled the walls.

Tillie's composure was rattled, too, but it broke down completely as she heard a suspicious noise coming from overhead. She looked up in time to see a stained and water-soaked acoustical tile sagging from the ceiling, apparently the victim of a leaky roof. Before she could move, the tile peeled away and dropped downward, hitting her squarely on the nose.

A stab of pain flooded her eyes with tears. She covered her face with her hands and turned her back to the employees, fighting hard not to scream.

Esther jumped up and pulled Tillie's hands from her face. "Are you hurt? Let me see."

Tillie imagined her nose turning into a purple plum.

Janelle appeared, holding a plastic bag filled with ice cubes.

Behind her, Tillie heard a shuffling of furniture and feet. Obviously, the meeting was over.

As it broke up, someone whistled and remarked soberly, "Construction is a dangerous game." Other choice comments drifted her way, including one that such a big, tough boss ought to wear a hard hat.

Tillie wished the ceiling tile had knocked her unconscious and they'd carted her off to the hospital. Instead, she had to suffer through the rest of the afternoon, replenishing her ice pack and being a good sport in front of the people she had tried to inspire to greatness.

She wondered to what or where she had inspired Austin. He wasn't around. He certainly didn't keep regular office hours. He seemed to appear from time to time, often wearing a tool belt that otherwise hung on a hook outside John Puckatt's old office. Then he would hole up in that office, absorbed by bar lists and placing drawings. Apparently, he'd taken it upon himself to do Puckatt's work in overseeing the day-to-day operations. He must have been working with the estimators, too, because somebody was doing the bidding, which Wallace used to supervise. She should get it straight exactly what he did. But this was only her second day on the job, and right now, her nose hurt too badly to worry about anything else.

Later, Robert Sandoval knocked at her open door.

"Jim asked me to speak to you about something," the shop foreman said.

"About what?"

"He wants a loan on his next check. Needs a couple of new tires for his car or he can't get to work."

Tillie remembered Jim out in the shop, remembered him as being like too many of the guys out there or in the field. They acted as if it were a given that they could blow half their check on liquor and still make it until the next payday.

"Maybe his girlfriend could drive him," Tillie suggested flatly. She had shown up one Saturday, a waif of a girl, stringy hair dragging over a low-cut blouse, wearing a skirt that could have passed for a sausage casing.

"This one doesn't have a car. Besides, I think it's more serious than the last."

"The blond gave up on him?"

"Hasn't been around in a long time," Sandoval said matter-of-factly.

Why should she worry about Jim and his latest fling?

"This girlfriend's been sick," Sandoval said. "Your uncle slipped Jim a few bucks once in a while."

That sounded like Wallace, generously taking on his employees' problems. Even though some weren't worth it, in Tillie's opinion, Kombardee Steel employees served as sort of an extended Kombardy family.

"He felt sorry for the girl. She's even had to quit her job."
Sandoval paused to make sure his meaning wasn't lost on Tillie.

"Okay, tell him to see Esther. I'll leave a check for him. Tell
him it's a gift."

The check Tillie wrote that afternoon to Jim was twice the
amount needed to buy two tires, although the checkbook balance was not as healthy as she would have liked. *I will think of
it as being for their baby,* she told herself, not a gift for two
people whose lifestyle is in direct opposition to my moral
standards. Besides, it was Wallace's money. Her uncle would
have helped an employee who was a needy father-to-be, and
while he was at it, probably would have conveyed a message
that he was sharing God's bounty because God loved all of
them. Tillie felt guilty.

As she closed the notebook-style checkbook and started to
put it in the safe for the night, the corner of a sheet of paper
worked its way from the back of the checkbook cover. She
opened to it and found a jumble of figures. Wallace had
hurriedly scrawled these notes, some of them running off the
page at the right margin.

Slipped into a pocket in the checkbook cover were copies of
the monthly financial statements for the past several months.
Wallace knew the company through and through. One glance at
an estimate and he would notice if the estimator had failed to
figure in the cost of some needed material. He could have
recited the balance due and the exact percentage of loan interest
being paid on that forklift that had broken down, Tillie thought
sadly. He always made his own written notes, translating the
numbers into his own simple arithmetic.

On one line of his notes, he'd written the letters *Inv* followed
by a figure with a lesser figure subtracted from that. The

difference was many thousands of dollars. Nearby was a question mark, thick and black and deeply imprinted in the paper, as if it had been traced over again and again. Obviously the two inventory figures had puzzled Wallace. Tillie wrote a note to herself, *Inventory,* prodded by Wallace's question mark to check into its deplorable state.

Near the bottom of the page were more scribbles boxed in by lines. Tillie turned the paper this way and that and decided it read *$50,000*. Also written inside the box was a word that looked like *Ernest* and the words *to be pd.*

She sure hoped somebody named Ernest didn't come around looking for his money.

six

Tillie dreaded going to the garage where she knew Dee's car had been towed after Wallace's accident, but she had to. The garage owner needed a signature to settle with the insurance company.

As she drove away from Kombardee Steel that afternoon, she gripped the wheel fiercely. She focused straight ahead as she passed the stretch of road where her uncle's accident had occurred, momentarily releasing one hand to pull down the visor against the low afternoon sun.

Once at the garage, she asked the owner if she could look at Dee's car.

He hedged. "Might not be the best idea. It's pretty well demolished."

"I think I should," Tillie persisted.

He led the way to a shed near the back of his property.

Tillie's first impression was one of dirt. The second was of the shattered windshield and the short space between the front seat and the dashboard.

"I wouldn't examine too closely, Ms. Gibson." The man moved to block her way as she neared the passenger's side.

"There might be something in the glove compartment we want."

"Oh, I cleaned all that out myself. Sent it over to the Kombardy house already. Put the stuff from the trunk in too."

Tillie wished Dee or Austin had mentioned that. But she still would have asked to see the car. Something about the terrible sight provided a strange reassurance, even as it tore at her

71

emotions. The twisted mass of metal, like a coffin, gave a sense of reality to the past week. She was living and breathing a true story, not a fictional horror tale. Wallace really was dead. She had to take his place.

"Just one thing," she said, turning away. "Was the car dirty like this when. . . when it was brought in?"

The garage owner became defensive as if she were suggesting that he hadn't taken proper care of evidence in an accident case. "Absolutely. We're careful about such things." Then, more kindly, he explained, "If you remember, there was a strong wind earlier that day, lots of dust. You can tell the windshield——what's left of it—was awful dirty."

As Tillie pulled way from the garage, she remembered the angle of the sun hitting her own car as she'd driven there. Poor Wallace. He always had been so particular about keeping the cars washed.

The next morning Tillie detoured by the shop before going into the office. Sandoval was checking crumpled papers on a clipboard.

"How's the workload?" she asked.

"About the usual."

She knew they had only two crews scheduled on jobs today, and the steel they would need should have been delivered to the sites before seven that morning. There wasn't much on the books for the next day either. A year before, weather permitting, the field crews totaled forty or fifty people, not today's skeleton crews. Her first task would be to find out if jobs were being properly bid and if the bids were going out the way they should. Over the noise of an old wooden stake truck lumbering through the gate, she told Sandoval, "We need a complete inventory of the stock."

He considered. "Guess we can do that. When do you want it?"

"This afternoon."

Sandoval frowned. "Have to do it when we aren't busy."

She refrained from laughing. The shop was hardly a beehive of activity.

Sandoval chewed the round end of his pencil, weighing the matter. "I guess we can at least start today."

"Good."

The stake truck had parked out in the yard some distance away. Tillie didn't recognize it or its driver, who stood with one foot perched on a bundle of reinforcing rods. He was talking with a couple of shop men. Jim was operating the bending machine. That made three men and Sandoval. Another man was out sick. Lots of payroll for little work, but what could she do, lay off somebody because work was temporarily slack?

She indicated the stake truck. "Who's that?"

Sandoval followed her gaze. "Scrap man."

There was always a scrap man stopping regularly to buy odd pieces of steel left after the rods had been cut to job specifications. Tillie went inside.

Esther's first words were, "We've got a problem."

"Just one?" Tillie tried to smile.

"Know that ten-thousand-dollar check we got yesterday from Olands?"

"Sure. I notice things like that." Tillie had gratefully taken it by the bank and made a night deposit.

"Well, the woman over at Olands called me first thing this morning. She put a wrong number on the notation she sent with the check and wants me to correct it."

Tillie idly thumbed through the telephone message slips Esther had handed her. "Did you?"

"Of course, but that's not the problem."

"What is?"

"The problem is twenty-two thousand dollars."

"What did you say?" Tillie's attention shifted rapidly away from the message slips.

"This Olands woman was chatting away about a zero balance. I stopped her short." Esther's chin went up. "They owe us twenty-two thousand more."

Ignoring a creeping ominous feeling, Tillie insisted, "It must be a mistake."

"Yes, and Olands made it." Esther had her fingers inside a folder, flipping through pages. "I just this minute pulled the job folder. I happen to know that the contract amount totals fifty-five thousand, not thirty-three. They've paid thirty-three."

"Did you tell her?"

"Sure. But she says their contract reads thirty-three thousand."

"Nobody would have the guts to try and cheat us out of that kind of money."

"This is a gutsy business," Esther said wisely.

Tillie knew that. But a discrepancy of twenty-two thousand dollars on a signed contract?

"Ah, ha. Here it is." Esther pulled out a white document, their standard contract. Her finger zipped down the right-hand side, stopping near the bottom. "Here it is. Fifty. . . ." Esther sputtered to a stop. "Hey. This can't be. I know that was supposed to be fifty-five. Wallace came up with that figure after a big discussion with the estimators and John Puckatt. Here, look at this and this." Indignant, she pawed through the folder producing evidence to support her declaration.

Tillie rushed around the desk to where Esther was about to hyperventilate. The contract did indeed read thirty-three thousand, both in numerals and where the amount was written out.

"Wait a minute! This is not my typing." Esther's acrylic nail jabbed the contract, and a degree of relief seeped into her voice. "I remember now. That was my vacation week. But I know it's wrong."

Tillie snatched the contract and took it over to where the morning light streamed in the window. She rubbed a finger lightly over the black numerals. There was a roughness to them. She examined the white paper and held it so the light filtered through. Suddenly she was conscious of Janelle sitting nearby and a detailer heating a roll in the microwave at Esther's wet bar.

She took the job folder from Esther's desk. "I'll see what I can do." She lowered her voice. "This is between you and me." Esther's only gesture was an intense frown.

Tillie shut herself in her office, utterly confused and angry. Someone had the audacity to use a whitening fluid to blot out part of the original numerals five and five and then go over them with a black pen to change them to threes. The typed words showed the lesser amount, evidently having been added after the correction fluid trick. Could anyone seriously think such an amateur job wouldn't be noticed? The word harassment crossed her mind, but that didn't make sense either. She buried her head in her hands. *Dear Lord*, she prayed silently, *what is going on? I'm just trying to do a good job, and these crazy things keep happening. I have to get this company on its feet for Aunt Dee's sake. Please clear my mind and give me patience and strength to deal with these mountains of problems.*

She heard an unusual commotion outside her door where the hallway led to the back half of the building. Shuffling feet, punctuated by grunts and groans, indicated that something was being moved past her office door with great difficulty.

"It goes in by the detailers," someone directed.

"Easy, there. Watch the corner." Austin's voice was sharp and clear.

Cautiously, Tillie opened her door. Two men carrying a heavy object nearly the size of a piano and wrapped in packing material edged their way by her.

An air of excitement had the detailers on their feet watching its arrival. As the procession reached its destination, the two estimators emerged from their office to observe the unveiling.

Tillie tried to catch Austin's eye but he was occupied. Rather than admit she didn't know about this momentous happening, she stood back and watched too.

As the movers peeled off the wraps, somebody whistled in admiration at the sight of a new, deluxe-model blueprint machine. After the initial hubbub died, Tillie summoned Austin into her office. She was more than a little disturbed. This was no time to be buying expensive equipment. Since he seemed to be master of ceremonies at the installation and also held the shipping papers in his hand, she fixed her frustration on him. "I see we have a new toy."

He rolled the shipping papers into a tube and rubbed his forehead with it. "You could say that. I'd call it an invaluable tool, one that's been needed for a long time."

"How much did this invaluable tool cost?" She held out her hand. He laid the shipping papers on her open palm with a bit of a slap. She went to her chair, reading as she walked. "Sit down," she told him.

"I'd better get out there. Want to make sure no one pushes buttons until we read the operating manual."

Irritated, she snapped, "Sit down."

He did so.

"I can't understand why Uncle Wallace would make a big purchase with the finances in the state they are."

Austin sat back and crossed his arms. "The old machine gave us nothing but trouble."

"I wonder if he looked into getting a used one."

"No, he didn't."

Tillie looked up in surprise. "He was always so practical."

"It was practical to get a new machine." Austin reached into a file basket on the corner of the desk, a basket Tillie hadn't yet touched. "This may answer your questions." He tossed a flimsy yellow sheet of paper on top of the shipping papers.

She recognized it as the file copy of a Kombardee purchase order form. Taking a closer look, she caught her breath at the dollar amount. Austin reacted by tilting his head back so he gazed at her through half-closed eyes. She picked up the page to return it to the file basket when the date on the form caught her eye. The purchase order had been written the previous Friday.

"Somebody ordered that zillion-dollar machine after Uncle Wallace died. Two days after."

"I did."

Tillie's eyes raced to the bottom of the form to the signature, *Austin Neff*. Below that, the space for title had been filled in with the words, *General Manager*.

"General Manager!" she exploded.

Her irritation seemed lost on him. "A matter of semantics. No one was using that title."

She swallowed her rebuttal in favor of the more pressing concern. "You just assumed we could pay for this machine?"

"I told you, we needed it. There was no choice. Can't operate this kind of a company without an operable blueprint machine." He looked up at the ceiling as if bored with the conversation, but Tillie could see his hands knotted into tight fists.

"It wasn't your money to spend!" she challenged.

"Perhaps not directly. Tillie, do you think you're the only one who has a stake in this outfit? Do you think you're the only one who cares what happens to it?"

"Couldn't you wait until. . . ." She almost said until Wallace was cold in his grave.

Austin stood abruptly. "No, I couldn't wait. We needed that machine as soon as we could get it." His boots pounded the short distance to the office door. "Excuse me. I have work to do."

Tillie moped a few minutes, consumed by frustration. Austin should have consulted her. Suddenly she realized that last Friday he must have thought that he was perfectly within his rights to make that decision. Last Friday he had assumed that he would be the one sitting at Wallace's desk.

On her return from a late lunch, Tillie again stopped at the shop to talk with Sandoval.

He shoved a wad of paper in a brown lunch sack, wiped his mouth on his sleeve, and tossed the sack in the direction of a waste container.

"How's the inventory coming?" She watched the crumpled bag bounce off the container and skitter across the floor.

The foreman stood up and waved a hand toward the yard, a flat expanse between the shop and the eight-foot chain-link fence bordering the side boundary of the property. A shop employee was standing between rows of bundled reinforcing rods stacked on dunnage and loosely grouped by length and size. "They're working on it."

She noticed a company truck driving out the main entrance. "Where's Jim going?'

"To get his tires."

She would rather Jim do personal errands on his own time. Sandoval's other man strolled along the old weed-covered loading dock toward the back of the property, too far away to count anything except the junk that dotted the landscape back there. This inventory seemed a slow process. She decided to take a closer look.

The sun shone brightly as she walked from the shop along the gravel drive that wound through the storage area. She began to perspire slightly. Her hair was cut in a short blunt style so it billowed out above her neck and curled under and forward over her cheeks. She brushed it back from her face, feeling the rush of coolness as the air touched her cheeks.

Being outside in this spacious yard far from sidewalks and tall buildings was a welcome change, even if the back section had become a dumping ground. She'd put the men to work clearing it out in their spare time.

Wallace had loved this place. Together they had paced off the perimeter, stopping to gaze at the mountains and maybe to aim a few rocks at a discarded hubcap. Working out of doors wasn't for her, but she could see other people thriving on it.

Near the middle of the plot, Tillie did an about-face, unable to resist taking a few moments to gaze at the scene that formed a backdrop for Kombardee's little realm. Fresh snow, dropped when the recent rains deluged Citrus County, draped across the rugged mountains. How wonderful God's plan was for His earth, she marveled. The snow pack, miles from here and thousands of feet up, provided beauty now and would yield fresh water in the coming dry season.

Long before she reached the first man assigned to do the inventory, Tillie began to wish she hadn't started this personal inspection. She didn't know these two people. They must be new at the shop. Her comfort level was sinking quickly. She should have let Sandoval handle it. With a false show of confidence, she marched up to the first man and asked to see his count.

He looked at her in surprise and handed over the clipboard. She made a pretense of studying Pierre's smudged figures. At least, that was the name written at the top of the clipboard. Not wanting to ask questions, she handed the clipboard back to the wiry man with the tight black curls. His count made little sense to her.

"Want to see Judd's?" he asked.

"That won't be necessary, thank you." She sized up the nearby bundles as if making an estimate of her own.

Tillie walked carefully back over the uneven ground. She'd already had an encounter with a snake and with a soggy ceiling tile. She didn't need to embarrass herself further by breaking an ankle in a gopher hole.

Near the shop she paused at the fabrication line where the rods were cut before being loaded on a truck for delivery to a job site. From the corner of her eye, she watched Austin come down the steps of the construction trailer and head for the office. She supposed he'd seen her poking around the yard.

After he was out of the way, Tillie wandered over to a sheltered area covered on top by a huge metal roof and enclosed on three sides by old truck trailers set on blocks. Wallace's beloved pickup was parked there, its gray paint now frosted with a thick coat of dust. The truck bed was empty except for the droppings of the local pigeons.

"Stupid birds!" she muttered, picking up a scrap of steel and throwing it as hard as she could through the open side door of one of the truck trailers. Clanging against the opposite wall, it bounced noisily on the floor. She was rewarded by an explosion of birds routed from inside. She marched back to the shop.

"Sandy," she said, "can you get the gray pickup washed this afternoon?"

"Sure."

"Esther has a set of keys. And can you have one of the guys clean up that place out there?" She indicated the shelter. "That pigeon dirt is revolting."

Immediately, she wished she'd simply told him what she wanted done instead of whining about the dirt. She tried to explain. "The truck trailers are useless in the shape they're in."

Sandoval screwed up his mouth as if studying a problem. Then he asked without emotion, "Which do you want first? The pigeon crud shoveled or the steel counted?"

His response was respectful enough, but Tillie knew she'd blundered. She answered, "The inventory," and fled to the office.

What was the matter with her? As a teenager, she'd had the freedom here to do and say whatever she wanted within reason. Upon becoming an adult, her age and gender drew invisible lines that separated her—the owner's niece—from the shop and field employees. Now a new dimension had been added: She had become the lady boss in a tough business.

She entered the outer office with a reserved greeting for Esther and Janelle that sounded more curt than she intended. Janelle's smile faded and the question in Esther's eyes stayed with Tillie all the way back to her office.

She badly needed an operations manager, someone to supervise the shop and the field men, someone to see that the work flowed smoothly from office to field. She flipped open Wallace's address file. A diagonal black line streaked through John Puckatt's address, crossing him off the Kombardee records. Nevertheless, she called and left a message for him to call her. He was well qualified to do the job, and she wanted to postpone looking for his permanent replacement. He'd been Wallace's top man for years. She must convince him to come back to work for a while.

seven

Tillie called Dee and suggested they have dinner together. Weary of leftovers, Dee came up with pizza. Their favorite take-out place was right on the way from the office to Dee's but Tillie had to keep another appointment first.

The Olands company president, albeit gruff, impatient, and on the defensive, let Tillie examine his copy of the contract in dispute. As far as she could tell, the Olands office was right. The contract amount was thirty-three thousand dollars, both as written in numerals and in words. Wallace had signed it. The fact that work done to complete the job was worth more than twice that didn't seem to bother the president.

He told Tillie, "I figured your uncle was underbidding just to get some work on the books and keep his crews busy, so I jumped on it. I would have been a fool to pass up that chance."

Tillie wasn't satisfied. She did know that Wallace had been forced on occasion to underbid jobs, choosing to keep his men employed rather than let them face idle days. Kombardee Steel absorbed the deficit. But she couldn't imagine him knowingly taking on a loss of that size.

At the Kombardy house, Dee seemed in fairly good spirits. Her friends had been telephoning and visiting, and someone was driving her to exercise class.

When Tillie took her final bite of pizza and wiped her fingers on a napkin, she asked, "Did Uncle Wallace ever mention anybody named Ernest?"

Dee put the leftover pizza into a plastic bag. "I don't recall that name." She carefully sealed the bag. "Here, you take this and tuck it in your refrigerator." At Tillie's objection, she insisted, "You need something you can just heat up when you come home tired and hungry."

Tillie finished clearing the dishes and loaded the dishwasher. Dee set out a plate of oatmeal cookies.

"I wish I knew more about what had been happening lately at the office," Tillie said, "with the books, especially. For instance, I'm wondering if you heard Wallace say anything about a contract with Olands. Like maybe there'd been a big change? Or maybe Wallace took the job below cost in return for a promise of more work?"

Dee frowned, considering her answer. She waved a cookie and said, "Wallace was the kind of man who left work at the office. He never talked much about it at home. Oh, lately, he'd tell me things about the people, some of it not too pleasant, but not about the accounts or contracts. Did you ask Austin?"

"This matter came up only today."

"Well, Austin might know. He was spending more and more time in the office. He even went in at night sometimes. He asked me questions, too, when Wallace wasn't around." She looked slightly embarrassed. "He wasn't snooping, understand. He simply realized that Wallace might be ill at ease about him taking such an interest."

After Dee's letters to Austin, her son might have come to Citrus County looking for problems. Wallace might well have become irritable over Austin suddenly poking his nose into company matters after a long absence.

Dee rubbed a delicate hand across her brow. "Austin worried about me, you know, even before this happened. I told him from the day Wallace and I married not to worry so much about my money. He's very protective."

Tillie gave a noncommittal, "Umm." She pursued another matter. "Anything new from the insurance company?"

Dee shook her head and looked away.

"We'll talk to Ralph Delanoy." Tillie hated to bring it up, but another item came to mind. "Does the name Lynn Lippincott mean anything to you?"

"Goodness, Tillie. I don't know her either."

"She's a CPA with Blackbourn."

Dee looked blank.

Tillie decided Dee should be told about this. "Her name is on the company bank account. She is authorized to sign checks."

Dee sat up in surprise.

"I met with Ms. Lippincott. She says that it was necessary to add her name to the account."

"I don't see why."

"I don't either, except for the payroll checks. Don't worry, I'm taking care of it."

A couple of hours later, Tillie gathered up the pizza and said goodbye to Dee. She climbed into her Ford and turned the key. No response. Exasperated, she tried again. The battery seemed completely dead. Refusing to give up, she tried once more. It was useless. She got out and vented her frustration with a fierce slam of the car door.

At that moment Austin's Explorer turned into the wide driveway that led to the garage and then on back to the guest house. Stopping beside Tillie's car, Austin emerged and asked the irritatingly obvious, "Car trouble?"

"It won't start."

"Want me to take a look?"

"Sure."

There was nothing in the conversation to indicate that

their last one had ended in an argument.

Dee came out to watch as Austin hooked jumper cables from one battery to the other. After an unsuccessful effort, Austin gave up. "It's not going to start. Must be something more than a dead battery." He unhooked the cables and began rolling them up.

Tillie turned to Dee. "Okay if I leave it here for now? I'll call the garage tomorrow."

"Certainly. I wish I had a car to loan you. . . ." Dee's voice crackled with emotion. She recovered and declared firmly, "Austin will take you home."

Tillie's mind raced. She hated to be without transportation, even long enough for the garage to check out her car in the morning. Suddenly she remembered Wallace's Chevy pickup, now a roosting place for the shop's pigeons. She didn't know how Dee would feel about turning her dead husband's truck over to someone else.

Before Tillie could make up her mind to suggest it, Dee exclaimed, "Why don't you drive Wallace's truck?"

Because Austin had to be at work before six-thirty the next morning, he agreed to drive Tillie to the plant right away. She could get the truck and drive it home.

When Austin turned the key in the ignition, the sound of a familiar Christian artist burst from the speakers. After driving a mile or so, Tillie still couldn't bring herself to ask Austin about the music. The fact that she had been a dedicated Christian while he merely tolerated her beliefs had been the major factor in their break-up.

She remembered vividly the summer of her college graduation. She had come home to find Austin living in the guest house, as he'd done most vacations and summers since Dee and Wallace married. Until then, she and Austin had been simply friends. But that summer their relationship exploded into a joyful, exciting romance.

They'd played tennis, walked moonlit beaches, hiked mountain trails, gone to major league ball games. Once she'd packed a picnic lunch and surprised him by driving him out to a canyon she had visited on a high school field trip. "All geologists like to look for fossils, don't they?" she'd asked. Together they toiled in the hot sun until, their skin caked with dirt, they traded tools for sandwiches and cold drinks.

One weekend they papered the bedroom in the guest house. Many Sundays they supervised Wallace as he barbecued chicken in the backyard, and they helped him build a brick walk from the patio out to the orchard. She'd wake in the morning and delay having breakfast until Austin came from the guest house, a gleam in his eyes and a kiss on his lips. Dee would smile knowingly and flutter to another part of the house.

Tillie turned her head toward the window, blinking back the tears. She realized now that their relationship had been bound for trouble. The Bible warned against being unequally yoked. Maybe if she'd been more patient and not tried so desperately to impose her views on Austin, maybe if she'd prayed more and talked less. . . .

"Tillie."

She jumped, startled by Austin's sudden intrusion into her thoughts. She tried to refocus on the present.

He repeated, "Tillie, I want to say something."

His tone was serious. He was probably going to tell her all the things she was doing wrong at Kombardee Steel.

"Yes, go ahead."

To her surprise, he broached the very subject that had

started her mind dancing through past dreams and desires.

"I just want you to know that," he said, reaching over to turn the radio off, "that I understand now most of the things you tried to tell me years ago. I know, too, why it was important to you that I hear them."

"Like what things?" she asked cautiously.

"Your faith in Christ."

Tillie caught her breath, a wild, unwarranted hope stirring in the far reaches of her mind.

He went on. "I guess some of the stuff you tried to drum into me stuck. A couple of other people got to me, too, to say nothing of what the Holy Spirit was doing in my life. At any rate, now that I'm a Christian, I can see why you weren't able to make a real commitment to a future with me."

So it was true, wonderfully true. A feeling of expectancy bubbled from some youthful dream that had been packed away like fine linens. Its sweet scent flitted from memory to memory, waking the dream and prodding it to new life. Tillie pressed the back of her hand against her quivering lips. *If only the change could have come when the love was alive,* she thought wistfully.

Austin slowed the car as if his words required more attention than he could devote while driving at high speed. "I can see now why you wouldn't marry me, why you insisted that your husband had to be a Christian. But I didn't see it then." He spoke the last sadly, as if in agreement with her unspoken thoughts. "You realize I was stubborn, and I didn't want to be told what to do or what to believe."

Tillie tested her voice. "I wasn't very patient."

New possibilities rose and fell in her mind like shooting stars. *Could there be a chance for her and Austin?* She canceled the unbidden thought immediately. She didn't even know how long he planned to stay. More importantly, someone could be waiting for him back in the Midwest.

They rode in silence. Now there was this new issue between them that could build into a fierce explosion: his mother's interest versus Tillie's in Kombardee Steel.

Still, out here in the dark, temporarily away from the office, they might find it easier to act naturally toward each other. She'd do her part to keep their relationship on an even keel. *For Aunt Dee's sake,* she told herself.

Tillie asked about the work he'd left behind. Yes, he still liked John Wayne movies. No, he never learned to play bridge, to Dee's regret. Yes, he still used the same tennis racquet. They spoke of playing again. He told her about the friend who'd taken him to hear an evangelist and how that godly man had spoken the words Austin needed, words that clicked with him and helped him go on to find a faith that was becoming deeper by the day.

"I'm so glad for you!" she exclaimed spontaneously and clasped his arm affectionately.

He responded with a warm laugh that sent shivers racing through her body.

They were nearing the plant when Austin pulled over and stopped. "Look, we've been on edge with each other. I suppose that's to be expected, being suddenly thrown together this way. But we can't let our emotions play havoc with everything we say and do. I propose a truce."

She looked down, not wanting to reveal the anticipation she felt. "Sounds good."

"We're both after the same goal," he said. "You want to rescue your uncle's company. That's exactly what I want too. I want to save Kombardee Steel."

Disappointment rocked Tillie at this turn in the conversation. "Why?" she blurted out. "You're in the geology business."

"For my mother's sake," Austin replied, a sharpness replacing the conciliatory tone he'd been using. "She invested her inheritance in it—all the money she had—when she and Wallace married."

Tillie had heard Dee speak of her inheritance during the early years of the marriage. Wallace always smiled gently, sometimes even winked. Tillie owed Austin an explanation. "I know your mother had some money when she married Wallace. But I don't believe there was any big investment in the company. Uncle Wallace never argued with her, but he told me. . . ."

Austin interrupted, "She's entitled to an income for the remainder of her life."

"The company will provide that."

"That company rightfully belongs to her."

"She owns half."

"Almost half," Austin corrected.

"She is happy with that. It's the way Uncle Wallace wanted it. He trusted me to take care of her."

"When it comes to honesty, I trust you too. But weird things have been happening. I think your uncle was a confused old man."

Tillie barely stifled a cry of anger. "How can you say such a cruel thing?"

"And I don't believe you're savvy enough or tough enough to deal with the problems at Kombardee Steel."

Tillie's rage burst loose. "Because I'm a woman, I suppose?"

Austin pounded the steering wheel. "Don't turn this into

some stupid male-female debate!" Abruptly, he started the engine. The tires ground noisily in place and then spun into action.

Tillie hated fights. She hated being hurt. The man sitting next to her was right about one thing. She sure wasn't tough. She straightened her shoulders and leaned hard into the back of the seat. But she would be tough about running this company because she had to be that way. Nobody was going to take it away from her until she was ready to sell.

Sell. It sounded so strange. *Sell. Sell!* She'd already made up her mind, hadn't she?

A single row of tall palms whizzed by, their tufts of foliage rising high above her view, their straight naked trunks standing guard over an abandoned vineyard that awaited the developer's bulldozer. If Wallace were here, he would know that selling Kombardee Steel was necessary. He had put her in charge of arranging a secure future for his wife. Selling was the way to do that.

They reached the secondary road that ran in front of Kombardee Steel. Austin braked and carefully made the turn from the main thoroughfare. Just as carefully, he said, "Obviously, we really need that truce. Shall we try again?"

Tillie was on such an emotional roller coaster, she could only mumble, "Truce."

Austin didn't pursue it. His concentration was drawn elsewhere. Already driving slowly, he tapped the brakes, at the same time flicking off the lights, easing his black vehicle along the dark two-lane road. It rolled past the entrance to Kombardee Steel before coming to a stop on the shoulder.

"Look," he whispered intently, pointing at something out the window on her side.

Tillie stared through the high chain-link fence. The

usual security lights posted at strategic points to flood the office doors and the other structures formed a pale cloud of light in the middle of the property. The shop area, however, partly hidden by one of the buildings, fairly pulsed with illumination.

"What is it?" Tillie whispered back.

A cryptic answer came from Austin. "Get down!"

When she failed to react quickly, he grasped her shoulder and pushed firmly. But before her head dropped below the level of the window, she saw the reason for Austin's alarm. Among the alien lights and shadows someone had invaded Kombardee Steel.

eight

Tillie heard the controlled click of Austin's door opening and the rub of cloth against leather as his body moved from the seat. He left the door ajar. She followed his footsteps by tracking the rolling crunch of gravel until they faded from her hearing.

Carefully, she eased her head up to where she could watch the scene inside Kombardee's fence. A quick movement back by the gate caught her eye. She knew that Austin must be working his way onto the property.

Her ears detected a familiar sound. At first, she couldn't place it, but then she recognized the whine of shop machinery. The shearer, with its powerful scissorlike jaws that cut effortlessly through steel bars, was raucous and threatening at close range but at this distance sang out soothingly.

She studied the scene intently, watching for signs of Austin and trying to find a clue as to the identity of the trespasser. She picked out a shape beyond the reach of the lights that might have been a car or truck.

The shearer shut down, its hum trailing off to a stop. Filling the silence came a discordant chorus of voices raised in disagreement. Tillie couldn't understand what was being said, but she didn't want to risk opening her door. She couldn't roll down the electrically operated window, so she climbed awkwardly across the seats to the driver's side. With one foot on the ground she was able to turn and look over the top of the Explorer.

The voices ceased. She gripped the door frame. Could the intruders have discovered Austin? Shrinking down, she wondered if her light hair might be visible against the dark background of the unlit road.

After an agonizing few minutes, the conversation at the shop resumed. Tillie sighed with scant relief and craned her neck. The shearer suddenly rumbled back into action. At the same time, a rush of steps came at her from behind. She bolted inside the vehicle and grabbed frantically at the door to pull it shut.

As the door was pried from her fingers, a voice hissed, "Stop! Don't slam it."

It was Austin. "Get over," he ordered.

Without giving her time to get out of the way, he shoved his arm past her and snatched the car phone.

She scrambled to her seat and huddled there, listening to Austin call the police. In the quiet that followed, he told her, "I found out why the inventory was so low."

"I knew it. Some contractor is stealing from our inventory."

"Keep your voice down. Not a contractor, employees."

"What?"

"Pierre and Judd. They're in the shop now, busily cutting up sixty-foot lengths of rebar into small pieces."

"Whatever for?"

"Know that guy who picks up scrap?" Austin's gaze traveled continually between the yard and the direction of the main street.

"The new scrap guy in the old stake truck?"

"Well, he's here now. Picking up scrap."

Tillie whirled to the window.

Austin told her, "You can't see him or his truck. It's parked over in the shadows. I heard enough a minute ago to know that hauling scrap away by the truckload is a frequent occurrence."

Out at the intersection of the road and the main street, two vehicles slowed, flicked off their lights, and turned toward where Tillie and Austin waited. As they neared, Tillie gratefully recognized the local patrol cars. Austin ran to the first one and then hurried to the main gate. Tillie held her breath as he pushed the heavy gate open, slowly at first, and then faster. But the machinery noise muffled the sounds of the gate's wheels rolling over the driveway. Austin jumped out of the way as the two patrol cars flashed their lights, turned on sirens, and sped inside. From somewhere came a third to block the entrance.

"How did those guys get in?" Tillie demanded as Austin returned. "Sandoval put a new lock on the gate today."

"We'll have to ask him," Austin said grimly.

Later Tillie sat shivering in the main office, thoroughly disgusted and completely puzzled. She could not remember ever being more angry than she was at this moment.

"Those rats! Stealing from me!"

Austin had called Sandoval. Now the shop foreman came in from the yard where he had been talking to a police officer. He wore what looked like a white flannel nightshirt printed with red hearts tucked in his trousers.

"I'm sorry about not locking the gate myself," he told Tillie. "I got a call about my kid and had to go. Then I guess I plain forgot. Ordinarily, I would have left Jim to lock up but he was already gone."

This didn't help Tillie's mood. She pictured Jim scooting off to his pregnant girlfriend instead of coming back to work after buying his tires, tires that she'd paid for.

"Apparently Pierre and Judd have been in the habit of supplementing their paychecks by creating scrap out of good rebar," Sandoval said. "They would cut it when they could and dump it out in the yard. Then this scrap guy would come and pick it up, like it was a regular pick-up." He fumbled with a clipboard someone had left on top of a file cabinet. "I guess no one noticed how many loads he hauled out of here." The clipboard clattered to the floor. The foreman ducked to retrieve it.

Tillie challenged, "And no one noticed the depleted inventory or that the scrap man wasn't even paying us scrap prices?"

The shop foreman squirmed. "I admit, there wasn't a good explanation for it. But I thought somebody cut down on the orders."

Tillie let him know what she thought of that weak excuse. "Isn't it your job to keep track of what's there and see that the office orders what's needed?"

"Yes, ma'am. We were taking an inventory today."

Tillie gave him a deadly look intended to remind him she'd been the one who insisted on doing that. She couldn't resist snapping, "An inventory taken by the two guys who were stealing us blind."

Austin had come in, accompanied by one of the officers. "Probably that's the reason for the big push tonight," he said. "Between the inventory and the new locks, Pierre and Judd figured they wouldn't have it so easy from now on."

Tillie stormed over to the coffee machine in an effort to hold her temper. She'd better cool down before saying more. She poured a quarter cup of stale coffee that looked like muddy gravy. She dumped it out in the sink.

"Tell me," she asked no one in particular, "how much were they getting for my steel? What's the going rate for scrap?"

The police officer answered. "Those two weren't exactly after money, Ms. Gibson."

"What?"

"They traded scrap for drugs."

"That scrap man is a dealer?" Tillie gulped. She wasn't so naive as to think none of the guys used drugs. "You mean they bought it right here, and paid for the stuff with my property?"

"Apparently that's what was happening tonight."

Tillie sank into the nearest chair. She had never felt so wronged, so exploited.

Sandoval approached her cautiously. "Now I wouldn't take it so personal." He stopped, testing her reaction. "Those two, Pierre and Judd, they haven't been here long. We'd have seen through them soon."

"We didn't soon enough," she countered, meaning that he didn't.

"There's plenty of good guys looking for jobs. We'll find some."

She had to accept that.

The office cleared out. Austin said if she felt like driving Wallace's truck, he would follow her to her apartment. She accepted, thoroughly depressed. She had to admit her spirits lifted slightly watching Austin's headlights in her rear-view mirror. As she opened her garage door, he gave a short tap on his horn and pulled away.

Tillie finally reached John Puckatt the next day.

"Sure, I can come in and help out," he said. "This retirement thing gets to be a drag sometimes."

They discussed the details.

Then he said casually, "I have already made some commitments. I'll try to get in for a while the first of next week, but I can't actually start until a week from Monday."

She put her elbow on the desk and leaned wearily on the hand holding the phone. "I really need you as soon as you can arrange it."

"I'll see what I can do. Be nice to get back to the old grind for a while. Just for a while, you understand," he said.

At least I'll have an operations manager that I can trust not to hover about wondering if I'm protecting his mother's interests, she thought cynically after she hung up. She heard Austin in the hallway buckling on his tool belt, getting ready to go out in the field, she supposed. *There was another advantage to working with John Puckatt*, she told herself. *I won't have to worry about falling in love with him.*

Before Austin left, he poked his head in her office and said, "I've contacted a guard dog service. They'll start Friday night."

"How does that work?"

"They bring by a dog after we leave Friday night. I'll take care of access for them. The dog stays here over the weekend, and they pick it up early Monday morning."

"Do they feed it?"

Austin looked disgusted. "No, they want it mean and hungry."

She wasn't sure if he were teasing.

"Of course they do. We call them ahead of time if anyone is going to work on Saturday."

"What about during the week?"

"I wanted to discuss that with you. They will do the same if we request it—bring a dog each evening and pick it up the next morning. But that rules out any night work."

"Hopefully, it would also rule out anything like what happened here last night."

"True." Austin shrugged. "Okay, I'll tell them every night, beginning this Friday."

After he left, Tillie went to Esther's desk to ask her to write up a memo and make sure everyone was aware of the new guard dog policy.

Esther commented, "Can that dog sniff out drugs?"

"I didn't ask," Tillie answered. "By the way, we will have some more help around here week after next. John Puckatt is coming back for a while."

"Puckatt? Puckatt?" The name popped out rapidly, making Esther sound like an excited chicken.

"Um-hmm." Tillie didn't want to discuss the pros and cons of her decision and turned to leave.

Esther slammed a desk drawer shut. "But your uncle. . . ." She let the words slip away.

Tillie waited for more.

Esther worked her lips. "I mean, Puckatt left because your uncle. . . , er, with your uncle's blessing."

From Esther's unhappy look, Tillie guessed that "blessing" wasn't her first choice of words. Tillie settled the matter. "It's only for a short time. We need the help."

As she walked away, Esther's grumbling complaint followed. "Got rid of him once. Can't he stay retired?"

Tillie passed Janelle, head down, pecking away at her keyboard, her eyes focused steadily on her hands. She gave no acknowledgment of Tillie's encouraging smile.

Lynn Lippincott came that afternoon and made herself at home at Janice's old desk. Tillie noted wryly that Lynn could type as efficiently as Janelle. In fact, the CPA seemed efficient at everything she did. Tillie was dumbfounded to find fresh, sparkling coffee at the wet bar, an improvement over the usual fare.

"Wonderful coffee," she told Esther.

Esther pointed a red nail toward Lynn's back and mouthed, "She cleaned the pot."

Tillie sputtered and swallowed the wrong way. Brewing coffee, much less cleaning the pot, seemed completely out of character for this woman wearing a several-hundred-dollar wool suit. Tillie stopped short of complimenting Lynn. Somehow kind words for performing such an ordinary task seemed inappropriate.

During the course of the afternoon, the accountant accomplished mounds of work. Periodically, she brought reports to Tillie's office and discussed them, after which she would say something like, "Of course, when we close out such and such, this will all come together."

Tillie felt ignorant asking too many questions and decided to wade through the material in private. She marveled at how thoroughly familiar Lynn Lippincott was with the financial workings of the company.

One sheet Lynn pulled off the printer was a projection of expenses for salaried employees. Tillie hadn't put herself on the payroll yet and Austin's pay wasn't shown. Being family members, they would be accessed by a special code.

Tillie did note a wage listing for the operations manager. Curiously, it was the same temporary rate she and John had discussed only that day, not a regular salary as he would have been earning before retirement.

That struck an odd note, and later when Lynn returned to Tillie's office, Tillie asked, "How well do you know John Puckatt?"

An indefinable look flickered beneath Lynn's dark brows. "Naturally, we came in contact with each other fairly often before he retired."

"Naturally," Tillie agreed.

"But as for being friends, no."

Tillie pursued the subject. "I notice you show a rate for operations manager." She wondered about the people whom Lynn would count as close friends.

"Yes." Lynn dragged a thick binder from between bookends on a table near the door and opened it. She ran a finger down the page, flipped to another, and scanned it. "I heard he was returning temporarily. Word gets around in a small office like this."

Tillie dropped it. Maybe she'd spoken too loudly during her phone call with John. Had she left her office door open? She may have told Austin, she couldn't remember. There was the possibility that John Puckatt and Lynn Lippincott did know each other outside of office hours. John in his eternal quest for youth and money paired with a CPA who probably already had a bundle but whose no-nonsense manner hinted that she'd skipped her youth entirely was an unlikely combination.

They worked quietly for a few minutes. Tillie stole a glance at Lynn who had taken a seat at the big table. A heavy silver link bracket dangled from one arm in a mannerly sort of way. Tillie was amused to see her using a fountain pen, the kind advertised to make a statement about the importance of its owner.

Tillie went to look over Lynn's shoulder. She realized she had never paid any attention to the set of thick binders stacked like building blocks along the table's inner edge.

Lynn sat back and replaced the cap on her pen.

Tillie stopped short of invading Lynn's space, but studied the pages from a respectable distance. "I'm afraid you'll have to fill me in on this. On my Saturdays at work, I never got as far as these."

The accountant picked up an inch thickness of pages and let them flip back into place. "They're simply the printouts for the year. Actually, they're of little importance, but they must be stored someplace. We have summary sheets in the files. That's really all anybody uses."

Tillie wondered if Wallace had understood them. He'd never mentioned them. He used his checkbook, his dog-eared ledger, the monthly statements, and his own notes. Occasionally he dug through the files for something he needed. Still, if the contents of this matched set of expandable covers were important, she should know. "They must have been generated for a reason."

Lynn snapped the binder closed as if offended. "Of course. These are a necessary step toward reaching the summary sheets." She pushed the neighboring volumes aside and sandwiched the one back into place. Consulting her watch, she stood up and said, "I have to leave. I'll finish what I was doing in the outer office first. That last file folder I gave you?" She pointed to where it lay on Tillie's crowded desk. "You might want to look at the top sheet. It's a memo I wrote to remind you of some matters that will be needing attention."

Tillie opened the folder.

Lynn spoke as Tillie scanned the page. "Quarterly tax report coming up. Then, there's the. . . ."

Tillie's startled gasp brought Lynn to a halt. "What's this?" Tillie demanded. "That last item." She read in a trembling voice, "Lease payment due." She snatched the sheet from the folder and moved it closer to the desk light. There were too many zeros in that figure.

Lynn's briefcase was open on the table. She patted and coaxed its contents into a neater arrangement. "Yes. The long-term lease on this property. Your uncle and the owner negotiated a deal, and the payment you see listed there is due in a few weeks." She closed the briefcase cover and firmly clicked the metal fasteners. "I realize the amount is sizeable, but the large lump sum payment is in return for the excellent terms. Mr. Kombardy agreed."

Still aghast at the amount of money due, Tillie asked, "Where's the lease? I want to see it."

"I believe it's in the safe." Lynn pointed to the framed landscape on the wall.

Did that woman know everything there was to know about

this place? Tillie wondered in frustration. "Why didn't my uncle tell me of such a. . . ," she floundered, unable to come up with the right word, "a momentous thing. Fifty thousand dollars! Where is that kind of money going to come from?"

Immediately, Tillie realized that she must sound like a whimpering child. She slammed the folder shut and said, "I'll look into this." She would strive for the same degree of dignity as the accountant. Tillie didn't want any more stunning surprises. She asked, "This is it? You have brought me up to date on everything?"

"I believe so."

Lynn surprised Tillie by closing the office door as a measure of privacy. "You may be wondering about my involvement in this business. I don't blame you for having questions. I have assumed a more active role here than in the ordinary accountant-client relationship. However, your uncle needed help, and I was the one he turned to."

A torrent of emotions—guilt, grief, and bewilderment—swept over Tillie. To Tillie's surprise, Lynn walked to where the small, square refrigerator rested on the floor. The CPA brushed the toe of her black leather pump against a cardboard file box that blocked the refrigerator door.

Lynn turned her foot as if checking to see if the dust from the box had soiled her shoe. It hadn't. "Take a look inside that refrigerator if you're wondering why your uncle welcomed my help. I don't think you understand the difficulty he was having. He was very proud and also quite protective of his wife."

Not waiting for Tillie to act, Lynn departed and closed the door behind her.

Baffled, Tillie shoved the cardboard file box away from the front of the refrigerator. The box was heavy, probably filled with more papers she wouldn't know anything about. She knelt, padding a spot on the floor with her full skirt to protect her stockings.

Tillie pulled a tissue from her pocket and polished the front of the refrigerator until the chrome handle shone. She tossed the tissue at the wastebasket and whisked her hands together. She was procrastinating.

The refrigerator must have been one of the last purchases Wallace had ever made. She pictured him lugging it in from his truck and unpacking it. She recalled his fondness for orange soda. She blinked back the moisture rushing to her eyes at the picture of Wallace indulging in his favorite treat and jerked the door open.

The contents were few indeed. A blue and white cardboard box and a small white paper bag rested on the shelf. No orange soda. Tillie pulled out the paper bag and started to peek inside it when she saw a coffee mug that had been hidden from sight.

She'd given the mug to Wallace because of the slogan written beneath a stylized sketch of mountain peaks. *God watches from the mountains.* Protruding out of the mug were a half-dozen plastic tubelike objects. Tillie snatched the mug with a jerk and stared in amazement at what she found: a supply of filled hypodermic needles, capped and waiting to be used.

Tillie tore open the paper sack and found a small bottle. Its prescription label indicated what she had already guessed. Wallace was not a borderline diabetic needing only to watch his diet. He was taking insulin and required regular injections that he must have been giving to himself.

The phone rang, startling Tillie so that she tilted the mug and spilled the needles. Looking warily toward the door, she unrolled a crisp blueprint and spread it face down like a tent, trying to cover the space in front of the refrigerator. She bolted for the phone.

It was Wallace's friend, Mack Swazee. "What a surprise," she managed to say, hoping that response would explain the tremor in her voice.

Mack had already sent warm notes to both Dee and Tillie, apologizing for being unable to attend the funeral. He asked, "Do you have a little time this afternoon? I'd like to come over."

She looked at the floor, wanting to refuse. Instead, she mumbled, "Sure, but could we make it kind of late?"

They set a time and the phone clattered into place. She dropped to the floor while convulsing into fierce, almost silent sobs. Wallace had borne alone the burden of advanced diabetes. Suddenly, she knew the reason for the deterioration in his handwriting, the clutter that filled the office, probably even the accident. His eyesight had failed rapidly and to a dangerous degree.

No wonder Wallace Kombardy had grown distrustful. He was becoming increasingly helpless to oversee his employees and to run his affairs.

She gathered the scattered needles. He had probably filled a supply of them, perhaps doing it unhurriedly in good light, to have them ready for use. Even so, the amount of insulin in them varied slightly, as if he'd been unsuccessful.

The enormity of his burden tore at Tillie's heart. She rubbed her fingers over the inscription on the cup. God did indeed watch from the mountains. As surely as He had heard Wallace's prayers, He would now be there for her.

nine

Tillie had just finished replacing the refrigerator's contents when a knock sounded at her office door. Hurriedly, she shoved the heavy file carton back in front of the refrigerator. For the moment, she would keep Wallace's secret hidden in the little brown cube. But how many others already knew it?

Austin entered, carrying a daily trade publication that Kombardee subscribed to as an important source of bidding information. The columns on its many pages were filled with listings of construction jobs out for bid. There were also bid results and building permits, as well as other industry news and advertising.

Austin pulled a chair around to Tillie's side of the desk and spread out the paper. "I was wondering why you didn't want us to bid on this reservoir." He edged the paper over so she could read it and ran his finger down a column to a listing she had not marked for bidding. "We have a good chance of getting that job."

She leaned toward him. The texture of the subtle blue plaid in his cotton shirt sleeve brushed against her skin. She moved her arm in a counter direction, straining to see the fine print. "We're losing money on the reservoir in Sibley," she said. "Let's learn from a bad experience."

"That Sibley job was delayed by rain, we were plagued with breakdowns of the delivery truck, and the shop messed up the tagging."

"Have to expect rain once in a while, breakdowns too. If we can't make money doing reservoirs, why do them?"

Austin moved to another listing. "What about this culvert? We do culverts all the time."

"I'm not sure we can handle it. The timing isn't right."

"We can get another crew together. Call in some of the guys who haven't worked for a while."

"I don't know," Tillie leaned back, her eyes on the wall calendar. "Maybe when we get more office help. I'm trying to get John Puckatt in here, but he's tying up loose ends or something."

At the mention of Puckatt, Austin stiffened and said sharply, "Have you thought of finding a replacement for him through the regular channels? Rehiring him could mean a replay of old problems."

"Care to elaborate on those old problems?" Between Austin and Esther, John didn't win many popularity points at this company.

"Just an expression. New blood could be a welcome change. Someone who would put the good of the company first."

"John didn't?"

"I didn't say that. I'm suggesting that someone else might tackle the problems here with a fresh attitude."

She frowned. Austin was pretty much doing the job now, but he was here because his mother asked him to come.

Austin transferred his attention to the scene outside the window, seemingly engrossed in the mountain range. His preoccupation gave her a chance to observe casually this man she had once loved so deeply. She remembered lying on the beach, counting the freckles on his handsome face, touching his skin warmed by the sun.

Her dark eyes moved quickly away as his blue ones darted from the landscape back to her. Embarrassed, she scooped up a pinch of paper clips and dropped them in the top right drawer.

It was out of the question to think of offering Austin the job as operations manager. What if he saw the proposal as a bribe to make him stick around? Worse, what if that were true?

Austin returned to the subject of bidding. "If we don't bid jobs, we don't get jobs. Without jobs, we don't make money."

"Of course. But why should we bid losers?"

"Small businesses have to take risks. I happen to think that small business is one of the most important segments in our economy, and it has the hardest role to play. The owners must live with risk every day in order to survive a myriad of regulations and labor problems and still operate at a profit."

He whacked the paper with his fingers. "Besides, these jobs don't have to be losers. If we can get our men working again on a regular basis, they're going to produce better for us. Some of them are having a hard time keeping food on the table. They get work where they can. Many prefer to work for us, but if we can't use them week after week, they go to the places that can."

"A few would have done us a favor by leaving."

Austin folded the paper and scooted his chair back where he could look at Tillie. "Sure, there are flakes in this business, but there are good workers too. Some are responsible family people."

Tillie's mind switched to Jim and his pregnant girlfriend. "That's just it. They are the ones responsible for their families. I'm not."

Austin sat in silence.

She squirmed at this new twist. Austin was endorsing Wallace's Christian concern. She admitted, "Oh, I know Uncle Wallace considered everyone here his extended family. But I'm not prepared to endanger this company's existence by providing jobs for the very people who would laugh at me for taking that risk in the name of Christian responsibility. Uncle Wallace made work when there wasn't work just to keep people on the payroll, and not for benefits the company would gain. That Olands contract is an example."

"Olands?"

"We must have bid a fifty-five thousand dollar job at thirty-three. I'd call that going to the extreme. They have a signed contract, and I don't think there's anything we can do about it."

Austin gave her an unreadable glance. "Mind if I check it out?"

"Help yourself."

"You know, Tillie, we are supposed to be good stewards of what God gives us. I mean, there is such a thing as witnessing for Christ by using material things we are blessed with to help others who haven't yet found Him."

She shot him a skeptical look. "That means a lot coming from a man who once ridiculed similar statements made by a Christian girl he called naive and pushy." She shook her head.

Austin's jaw stiffened. He took his chair and recklessly planted it back in its original spot, grinding the legs into the floor. "Well, you were pushy. Kept trying to shove your didactic edicts down my throat."

Tillie didn't want to get into that. "Austin, I know I made mistakes the other time." She knew that sounded wrong. But what was going on between them now seemed like a repeat of what went on before. She stood and faced the window. Her heart pounding, she gave in to her feelings. Maybe it was true, maybe she was falling in love with Austin, again. Maybe she'd never fallen out of love. "That is, I suppose I was pushy." She whirled around and confronted Austin. "But I wasn't naive about my faith!"

Austin took a step toward her, and her heart seemed to stop pounding, or beating at all.

"No, your faith was strong, as it should have been. I'm the one whose faith was weak. Absent would be a more apt description. And I was too stubborn to listen to you tell me the truth." He had moved closer, his hands inching upward, then dropping back, as if fighting some private tug-of-war.

Just then the phone rang. Together they stared at it through the second and third rings. Finally, Tillie shook herself into action, settling into her chair while trying to find the perfect pencil. On the fourth ring, she fumbled with the receiver.

Tillie asked the caller to hold, placed her hand over the mouthpiece, and silently waited to see if Austin had more to say.

To her surprise, he extended an invitation. "Come with me tomorrow out to the field." It was more than an invitation. It was a plea.

"Whatever for?"

"Have you visited a job site lately?"

She shook her head.

He turned to go. "Well, then. Tomorrow morning. I'll pick you up at your place at six sharp. Bring your hard hat."

She watched the door shut after him. There wasn't much point to her tromping around a construction site. Still, the prospect of an outing with Austin had attractive overtones, especially when she considered that he could have suggested they meet at the job site. But he hadn't.

Mack Swazee sat across from Tillie's desk. His broad face wore a kindly look that belied the sun-weathered skin and the sturdy body of a man who had spent more than half of his forty-five years working in the construction industry. Tillie leaned back in her chair and, in one of the few moments since Wallace's death, thoroughly relaxed. Mack and Wallace had been friends for many years. Having him there was a little like having

Wallace around.

They made small talk for a while. She imagined Mack Swazee beginning in the field, working his way up from crew member to foreman, and eventually starting his own company, as Wallace had done. Mack had been in concrete block construction and not in competition with Kombardee Steel.

Despite the hardiness required of any man who would run a rigorous, demanding, low-margin business, Mack, like Wallace, had not forgotten how to be a gentleman. Clad nattily in his knit shirt and trousers, his blond curls touched with gray, he conversed with confidence and ease. The exchange offered Tillie an immeasurable amount of simple pleasure and the reminder that this construction world had its good points. Wallace had always claimed that, but of late, the minuses in the industry seemed to far outweigh the pluses for Tillie.

Soon, though, Tillie's warm, secure feelings toppled. Mack casually rubbed the back of his neck and eyed her from beneath heavy blond brows. "Wanted to talk a minute about the sale."

She didn't have a clue as to what he meant. On guard, she imitated his nonchalant style and asked, "Sale?"

Mack's face closed a degree. He raised one ankle and propped it on the opposite knee, holding it in place with a firm handclasp. The ring finger on his left hand was shorter than it should have been. She remembered that the tip had been sheared off long ago in an industrial accident.

He cleared his throat. "The company. Wallace and I had done some strong talking."

The chair beneath Tillie seemed to drop away and then catch her with a jolt like the seat on a carnival ride. She grabbed its arms. "Talking about what?"

A note of anxiety entered Mack's voice. "We had a deal going before. . . before your uncle died." Apparently offering proof, he added, "Sort of a handshake deal, I admit. But there was a deposit."

"Uncle Wallace was going to buy your company?" Tillie exclaimed in disbelief.

Mack jerked upright, slamming his foot back to the floor. "No, no. You've got it wrong. It's the other way around. I'm buying Kombardee Steel."

The idea that Wallace would sell his beloved company was preposterous. She reined in her surprise, trying to assimilate this news. Mack had been Wallace's friend. She would expect the truth from him.

Mack pulled out a white handkerchief and swiped it across his brow. "That is, we were in the process of me buying this place. I supposed you knew. Don't understand why he didn't mention it, so you could get used to the idea."

Mack was right. Tillie needed time.

"Actually," he continued, "I was surprised myself when Wallace proposed the notion."

"My uncle approached you? Asked if you wanted to buy Kombardee?"

Mack nodded emphatically. "The more I thought about it, the more I liked the prospect. I'm working with the bank. But you know how slow those suit-and-tie fellows can be."

Tillie swiveled the chair, her glance roving aimlessly over the room until it hit on the small brown refrigerator and its secret. Yes, remembering his deteriorating health, she could picture Wallace seeking a buyer, and the first person he would have approached might well have been his old friend, Mack Swazee.

Mack was still commiserating over bank regulations. "They want as much paperwork as the government. Go to fill out a loan application and you'd better remember what you had to eat for breakfast on Lincoln's birthday two years ago."

She said, "I suppose you had to supply information on us."

"Of course." He gave her a quizzical look. "Everything's still the same, isn't it? Nothing has changed lately, has it? Except. . . ."

She finished for him. "Just the change in ownership."

He looked worried. "Tillie, your uncle wanted me to have the company. And I want it. I hope there's no problem with that."

She didn't answer. A thousand thoughts swirled in her mind.

Mack wadded up his handkerchief and replaced it in a hip pocket. "I'll get going. I'm sorry about surprising you that way. I supposed you and Dee both knew. Let it sink in a while. You'll see it's for the best." He got to his feet and adjusted his belt.

"What about the employees?"

"Don't worry. Part of our agreement was for me to keep everyone on. Wallace was specific about that. He didn't care so much about the facilities. At least, not lately." Mack leaned his big hands on the desk. "You know, Tillie, Wallace was tired. Awful tired."

Mack's next words came softly but surely. "Completing this deal that your uncle started would solve a lot of your problems."

Tillie bit her lip to keep from crying.

Tillie decided not to mention the sale of Kombardee Steel to Dee right away. A telephone conversation on such an important subject didn't seem appropriate, and she was so exhausted that night that to heat a plate of leftovers in the microwave seemed an overwhelming chore. No, she'd wait and tell her aunt in person. She'd wait to tell Austin too.

Although Tillie had earlier plucked the idea of selling the business from the morass of shadows haunting her since Wallace died, the reality of cutting loose the entity that had been like a child to him was another matter. Tillie knew the business should be sold, but she needed to have her own emotions firmly under control first.

She went from the kitchen out to the garage and opened the dryer door. The load of clothes had been dried the night before and the wrinkles were set. She turned on the air again.

While she waited, she lifted the flaps of a sectioned carton that held a half-dozen potpourri jars and let her eyes feast on the glistening crystal topped with covers of elaborately filigreed pewter. She removed a cap and imagined the jar filled with fragrant dried leaves and blossoms. Business inventory could be more aesthetic than stacks of reinforcing steel with various deformation patterns of ribs and codes.

The next morning Tillie dressed in jeans. Under a matching denim jacket, she wore one of her most flattering blouses, a long-sleeved forest green silk shirt. She chose button-type sterling earrings. She told herself that the silk shirt and earrings had nothing to do with Austin's presence. To prove it, she went out to the garage and hunted up an old pair of boots. Any illusion of being overdressed would be instantly dispelled.

Wallace's truck occupied the only available parking space in the garage. Her car now spent most of its time in an outdoor parking slot. She got her hard hat from the front seat and went back to eat a quick bowl of cereal before Austin came.

He was five minutes late, she noticed, as she paced in front of the living room window. Maybe she should drive the truck, so they could go their separate ways after she'd satisfied this notion of his that she should visit the field.

The doorbell finally rang. When she got herself collected enough to answer, he greeted her with a simple, "Ready?"

She locked the door and they went down the walk together.

"Kind of like the old days," he remarked, "except that this time I had to leave home to pick you up."

Her heart raced as she told herself to stop making a big event out of this. "No curfews, either," she answered.

Chuckling, he opened the passenger door. "Oh, yes, the curfew. You're the only girl I ever dated who had a curfew."

He climbed in, a grin lifting the corners of his mouth. "You know, I always felt funny about the way your uncle and even my own mother protected you from me." He started the engine. "I never understood it. It was as if neither one of them completely trusted me."

"Don't be silly."

"Well, as it turns out, one of them sure didn't."

At that moment a chilling realization raced through Tillie's mind. Wallace might indeed have kept Kombardee Steel out of Austin's reach because he could not trust him.

With that sobering thought, the prospects for a lovely outing dimmed into nothing more than a dutiful inspection trip to a job site, probably half-buried in mud from the recent rains. She'd do her best to show interest while trying to stay out of the way. The field crew would tolerate her presence, and she would tolerate their pretense of clean language and superhuman efficiency.

ten

Their destination was the site of a storm drain being built in a channel that ran through a residential neighborhood in Brogerston. Austin stopped on the way at a partially completed parking structure across the street from a large hospital.

"Have some dobies in the back that didn't get fabbed in time to get on the truck," he explained.

Austin hoisted the short bars angled on one end and took off. Tillie got out and followed, stepping around a bundle of long reinforcing bars on the ground. She paused to examine closely the marks on the bars, trying to recognize the deformations.

The deformations, or lugs, on this kind of bar served as ridges to allow the newly poured concrete to grip the bars better and prevent slippage. In addition to the ridges, other deformations formed symbols. The symbols identified certain properties of the reinforcing rods.

In times past, she used to try to show off for Wallace. She'd take a quick look at the deformations and then recite the bar's diameter, the grade of the steel used, and the name of the mill that had produced it.

These particular bars had been cut back at the shop to a specified length. Her guess was twenty-four feet. Then they'd been put through the bending machine.

"Type one bend?" she asked Austin, sure that she was correct about the shape.

Without stopping, he accused, "You read the tag."

"I did not." But now she bent and inspected the stiff computer bar tag attached to the bundle. "I was right!" she announced

115

gleefully. "Even got the exact length."

She caught up with Austin as he reached the job foreman. She stayed with the two of them for a while, then wandered back toward the Explorer, speaking to any ironworker who glanced her way. Austin was right that she should show an interest in the field work.

She reached the edge of what would be the ground floor of the parking structure. The early morning sun played across the bars that had already been placed in a huge expanse of precisely arranged reinforcing steel, a gridiron of strength awaiting the pouring of concrete. The pattern formed had been strictly dictated, she knew, by the placing drawings that a detailer had prepared from the engineering drawings.

She was fascinated by the pattern of light and shadow in the sculptured steel carpet before her. The repetition of the neat squares of textured bars, tied at intersecting points and propped up a precise distance from the surface below, was pleasant to the eye.

Clusters of upright bars marched in formation at carefully spaced intervals, forming the framework for what would be supporting pillars for the second floor. She watched ironworkers construct the skeleton, stopping now and then to stand back and survey the task from a distance. For the first time, she saw the ironworker as a skilled craftsman, and ironworking a demanding craft requiring consummate precision.

Although the temperature was chilly, most of the men had already shed outer layers of clothes and worked in tee shirts. Heavy tool belts were strapped over their jeans. Such standard equipment as a spool of wire inside a metal container and wire cutters in a leather pouch dangled from the belts.

Tillie took off her hard hat and fluffed her hair as Austin came her way with a surefooted stride. Somehow Austin looked at home here.

As they drove on to the next job, an idea repeated itself in her mind. Perhaps if she and Austin cooperated, they could get this company going. Could she count on him for help, real, unselfish help?

She nibbled on a blueberry muffin that he'd bought from a catering truck back at the site and watched him from the corner of her eye. They'd nearly been a team once, and they both wanted the company to succeed, but for vastly different reasons.

Abruptly, Austin made a sharp turn from the smooth pavement onto a dirt construction road. Tillie was jolted from her daydream. She popped the last of the muffin in her mouth and resolved to get back to the real world. Austin had not given the slightest indication that he was anxious for any kind of partnership with her.

As they got out and walked toward the job site, Tillie asked, "You were going to look into the discrepancy on the Olands contract. Any results?"

"Still working on it," Austin replied and picked up the pace.

Their path rapidly narrowed into a dirt ledge about two feet wide, making it necessary to walk single file. Close to the right ran a wooden fence that served as the rear boundary of a string of large backyards, part of a suburban community. Over the fence could be seen trees and the upper reaches of an occasional child's gymset. Immediately on their left was a huge open flood control channel. Beyond that lay a stretch of vacant land being graded for construction, probably apartments.

The covered storm drain under construction in the channel was being finished in sections. The completed part resembled a train of windowless boxcars glued together end to end and running along the channel below the level of the dirt ledge. After they passed the completed section, Tillie and Austin came to where the Kombardee crew worked. Here the bottom and sides of the drain had been finished in concrete. The crew swarmed over a maze of supports, placing closely spaced reinforcing bars across the top. Next would come the concrete layer that would form the permanent cover for the drain.

Tillie paused to watch the crew work. The upper edge of the finished concrete side was barely wide enough to accommodate work boots. Ironworkers traversed it easily, using it as a platform from which to lean over the flat upper surface and tie bars. Some men stood, bent double at the waist, on boards laid across the unfinished top. One man knelt on the top and hung down headfirst over the outside.

Wooden forms, scraps of lumber, and buckets dotted the structure. A heavy rope draped from the drain over to the dirt ledge where Austin and Tillie walked.

Austin stepped around the rope. A piece of scaffolding, a single board about fifteen feet long with tacked-on treads, lay on one end on the dirt ledge and the other on the drain. The chasm below it formed a wedge with the steep, rocky embankment on one side and the drain's concrete side on the other. Down at the point of the wedge lay a jumble of construction debris. Austin tested his way out on the scaffolding.

Determined to follow, Tillie waited until he was a few feet ahead and then stepped on behind him. But instead of completing the crossing, he paused. Tillie, hurrying to keep her balance, bumped into him just as he turned around toward her, a scowl on his face.

They teetered precariously while clutching at each other. She squealed and he yelled a useless, "Watch out!"

She was conscious of shouts and a flurry of motion over on the concrete drain, and her panic was peppered with fleeting visions of broken bodies at the bottom of the wedge. *Please,*

Lord, not a cave-in! she prayed frantically.

Like high wire performers, the couple kept their footing for moments, the board beneath them swaying unpredictably until gravity won out and the two of them toppled to one side. The scaffolding flew from beneath their feet.

Tillie felt a brief sensation of free fall, with herself and Austin falling as one. A sudden, neck-twisting jerk brought them up sharply. Austin's arm across her back pressed against her ribs and under her arms. She dangled in midair, suspended by his hold on her as together they swung toward the sloping dirt side of the scooped out channel. Now the arm pressed into her back with the power of a baseball bat, and the weight of Austin's body hit her full force from the front, as first she, then he, slammed into the hard dirt.

He rolled to one side, still supporting her weight with his left arm. She tilted her head upward to see what miracle had kept them from dropping fifteen feet or so, wedging themselves into the v-shaped space below where the bottom of the stony dirt channel met the rigid concrete structure.

Looking past Austin's strained face, Tillie saw his right arm raised upward with his hand around the rope that had previously draped across the chasm. He had caught it as they fell and now clutched it in a tenuous grip. Even as she watched, the rope slipped, and his fingers slid agonizingly down the rough fibers. Holding her as he was, it was impossible to secure his grip by wrapping the rope around his hand, and the lifeline continued its slow crawl from Austin's grasp.

Through clenched teeth, he grunted, "Grab the rope!"

Caught between obedience and the fear of tearing herself from Austin's hold, Tillie felt for the loose end and closed first one hand and then the other around it. At her nod, he released her long enough to improve his own grip.

Would the dirt embankment give way and swallow them up, buried alive? Tillie wondered desperately. *What secured the rope they clung to?*

She looked up in alarm at a dull thud overhead. A wide board, still vibrating from the impact, had been thrown from the top of the storm drain, spanning the gaping chasm. A burly ironworker darted across this new bridge, his weight bowing it so that Tillie thought it would surely break.

From the dirt ledge came his reassuring voice, "The crazy rope is caught on a piece of buried cable. Don't worry, I've got a good hold on it now."

Two men, slipping and sliding, had scrambled over the side of the drain and were now below Tillie and Austin. They rescued the scaffolding and were propping it against the bank beside Tillie. One of them inched his way upward until he reached her. She pried her hands from the rope and let him help her twist herself onto the scaffolding. Legs trembling, she climbed as high as the treads would allow. A welcome pair of dirty hands reached from above and pulled her to safety.

Austin followed, breathless, his right palm caked with blood and grime. He gingerly flexed his arm.

When the drama was over, Tillie tried to thank the men. Thinking quickly, they had acted unhesitatingly to avert what could have been a serious accident. She was shaken, and the words did not come easily.

Later, similar words of appreciation stuck in her throat when she attempted to apologize to Austin for her careless action. "You were just turning around to tell me not to do what I did, when I did it, weren't you?" she asked awkwardly. He'd received first aid for his hand, but she insisted on driving him to an emergency care center to have a professional look at the damage.

"Watch where you're driving. This is my car," he scolded.

"I am. But I'm nervous." She didn't blame him for being angry.

They pulled into the parking lot at the medical center. She let the motor run, wanting time to talk with him before he got out. "Austin, I know I acted impulsively back there, and we both could have been hurt, seriously hurt. I'm sorry, and I appreciate the way you kept me from falling down into that crevice." Finished, she shut the motor off and unbuckled her seat belt. "Wait, and I'll come around and get the door."

"I'm not crippled—quite," he muttered, and then lashed out, "You could have been killed. Don't you ever pull a trick like that again."

Already on edge, Tillie dropped the keys on the floor. She had maintained a shaky composure until that moment, but now she was ready to cry. She ducked down and felt around on the floor for the keys. Even after she found them, she kept her head lowered, blinking madly, trying to forestall a fit of hysterics. Her clothing was torn, dirt frosted her hair, and her back hurt from the blow received when she and Austin swung against the bank. She told herself that he had a right to yell at her, but she didn't like it.

Keeping her face averted, she scrambled out the driver's side and went around to Austin's door and opened it. He felt for the button to release his seat belt. She leaned across unfastened it for him. Wordlessly, he climbed out and went inside.

"Have them take x-rays," she called.

Waiting for Austin, she became more than ever convinced that selling Kombardee Steel was the only path she could reasonably choose. Mack Swazee had said the employees would be kept on. A rush of emotion swept over her at the thought of the ironworkers back at the storm drain. For the first time in years, she put faces with the names on the payroll.

Wallace, of course, knew everyone personally.

Tillie began to cry in earnest. She hadn't ever bothered to see these people the way Wallace did. Instead, she saw their IOUs and heard their coarse language. She always considered herself fairly tolerant and compassionate but she wasn't, not really. Wallace had loved his employees, as God would want him to love them.

Her head bent over the steering wheel, she was startled to hear a tap on the window. Austin stood there, holding up a cleanly bandaged hand for her inspection. He motioned her out.

She dabbed at her eyes and opened the door. "What did they say?"

"It's nothing. I'll drive."

She walked around to the other side, trying not to favor any of the parts of her anatomy that were beginning to show signs of trauma. She regulated her breathing, afraid that a deep expansion of her lungs would make her back hurt. She should have gone inside to see a doctor but she didn't want to cause any more trouble than what Austin already knew about.

She felt his gaze on her as she climbed in the passenger seat but he kept his thoughts to himself. She dug in her purse for a comb, wishing she'd hunted up a place to wash her face. He looked like he'd done that.

The route back to Tillie's apartment led by the parking structure where they had stopped earlier.

"Have to stop here a few minutes," Austin told her. "Will you be okay?"

She nodded. While he conferred with the foreman, she sank back and watched the scene before her. It was nearly eleven o'clock now and the iron grids and pillars formed more of a mundane picture than they had in the slanting rays of the early morning sun. This was the real picture, she told herself, one of work well done. Wallace would be proud of this job.

All of a sudden, she wanted to be a part of it, of the construction business. How could she even think of selling the company when Wallace had entrusted it to her care?

When Austin returned, she reached over and stopped him as he inserted the key in the ignition. "Can we talk a minute?" she asked.

"Sure, but I thought you'd be anxious to get home."

"I want to ask you something."

He waited.

"I've decided to try my best to build Kombardee Steel back up to where it once was."

"I didn't know you had any other objective."

She wondered if the guilt that rushed over her showed. He couldn't know that Swazee wanted to buy the company and that less than an hour earlier she saw that as her salvation. "I mean, I'm going all out to correct the problems that we have, to keep the crews employed, to make the best use of our resources. I know the company can be turned around."

His blue eyes studied her, but she didn't meet their gaze for long. She massaged the cuticle on a nail, smoothing away dirt from their morning's adventure.

"Austin," she said, surprised at the tremble in her voice. "I want you to help me—really help me—build Kombardee Steel back up to something that would please Uncle Wallace."

Austin played with his keys. "What about you? Would that please you, Tillie?"

She caught her breath. She had just realized the great extent to which that would please her.

But he continued, "I mean, to have the company be a going concern with you at the helm?"

"I'd need people I can trust around me," she said carefully.

"The boss lady could use a partner." She tried to chuckle but didn't succeed very well.

"Tillie, I'm not sure."

"About the partner?"

He pulled on the steering wheel and shifted his weight. "Well, about any of this. I want to improve the business, to make it turn a profit. Why do you think I took it upon myself to order that blueprint machine? Why do you think I brought you out here today if it wasn't to let you see that the crews are still capable of performing if they get the jobs? But as for you spending your days out there in the boonies surrounded by reinforcing rods and rough-talking guys—well, wouldn't that get old? What about your own plans?"

"You don't understand. I think this is what I should be doing. I owe it to Uncle Wallace and to your mother, and to the employees. Besides," she groped for words, "I don't want to let it struggle on in a halfhearted way. This company has been a part of my life for so many years, and now, the thought of not giving it every bit of my energies and abilities seems wrong. I want to turn it around. Will you help?"

Austin jammed the key in the ignition. Over the roar of the motor, he said, "I'll help you."

As they sped away from the site, Tillie felt a surge of elation at the prospect of the two of them tackling the challenge together. At the same time she realized with foreboding that Austin's commitment went no further than getting the company on the right track.

As Austin escorted Tillie to her door he advised, "Maybe you should take the rest of the day off."

She watched him pull away and realized for the first time the dilemma she faced. She loved Kombardee Steel, but she loved Austin Neff more.

eleven

Swathed in a white towel, Tillie twisted to view her back in the mirror. She was looking for bruises and trying to convince herself that she shouldn't return to the office that afternoon when the telephone rang.

Esther reported, "Mack Swazee called. He was kind of perturbed not to find you here."

"Did he say what he wanted?"

"No, except he thinks it's important."

Tillie breathed deeply, testing for rib damage. No problem. She did a shoulder roll, expecting pain at any second. It was no use. There wasn't anything wrong with her. She conceded wearily, "Call him back. Tell him I'll be there at one o'clock."

Sighing, she pulled a black denim skirt and jacket from the closet and slipped on a turquoise blouse. How do you tell someone that you want to cancel a deal between old friends presumably made with a good-faith handshake?

Precisely at one, Mack Swazee walked into the front office. Tillie heard his heavy step even before she heard him boom, "I'm here to see Tillie."

Esther, evidently in a contrary mood, told him, "Have a seat. I'll see if she's available."

Tillie waited while Esther took her time meandering to her office instead of picking up the phone and buzzing.

Esther tapped lightly on the door frame, stepped in, and said officially, "Mr. Swazee is here to see you." Then she winked and whispered, "He's hot under the collar, but I'm letting him cool his heels a bit."

"Thanks, Esther. Send him back."

Tillie closed the door after Mack entered. He seated himself in the chair opposite her desk, showing signs of being an unhappy man.

After a polite interlude, he jumped right in. "I know now why those bankers have been stalling about this deal to buy Wallace's company."

"What do you mean?" Tillie noticed the reference to ownership but forgave him.

"I mean that I'd still be waiting around and nothing would be happening if a friend of mine at the bank hadn't run onto an interesting detail."

A shiver of alarm rippled through Tillie.

Mack's tone softened with a sympathetic note. "I'm sure it's not your fault. But," he declared emphatically, "I don't like surprises when it comes to business deals."

Tillie was sure she didn't either.

He rubbed his jaw thoughtfully. "Did you know that there is a big lease payment due on this property?"

Tillie nodded.

"Well, that makes a whopping difference."

"In what way?" A glimmer of hope rose in Tillie.

He obliged zealously. "There's fifty thousand dollars due to your landlord a few weeks from now. Don't ask me how Wallace got roped into such a deal, but my friend at the bank tells me that's the way it is."

Tillie suggested, "I understand that Uncle Wallace signed a lease that included a lump sum payment in exchange for excellent terms."

"No lease is worth that. The thing is, Tillie," Mack's voice was almost apologetic, "Wallace and I agreed on a price, and there was no mention of any outstanding debts like that." He stretched his chin upward and fastened the top button on the placket in his knit shirt, then promptly unbuttoned it. "So, you see, the price I was willing to pay Wallace didn't include an extra fifty-thousand encumbrance."

"You mean, we're fifty thousand dollars apart in our negotiations?" Tillie toyed with a string of paper clips.

"What negotiations?" Mack's question bordered on aggressiveness. "Wallace and I agreed on a price, and I paid him a deposit. He wanted cash, and I paid it. Made me awful nervous to do it but he gave me a receipt and I knew Wallace was a man of his word."

"Cash? How much cash?"

"Kind of a coincidence. Fifty thousand."

Tillie dropped the paper clips. "Fifty thousand!"

Mack paled. "I assumed you knew."

A mention of a deposit from their last conversation came to Tillie.

"I've got the receipt," Mack repeated.

Silence followed. Tillie's spurt of elation at the prospect of Mack wanting to cancel the purchase fell flat. Could a deposit of that size be missing? If Mack could come up with a receipt, she'd have to return his fifty thousand dollars if she didn't sell. What a coincidence that that was the exact amount owed to the landlord.

Obviously disturbed, Mack said, "There must be a record of what Wallace did with that cash. He wouldn't just fritter it away, even though. . . even though lately he wasn't quite his old self. I'd guess that he paid off the landlord early if I didn't know better."

Trying not to appear as stupid as she felt, Tillie assured Mack, "I'm not arguing that you gave my uncle a deposit. I just wish you two had written up an agreement."

"We'd have gotten around to that." Mack eyed Tillie warily. "You managing this outfit okay? Do you have a good handle on the books?"

"Pretty good," Tillie said defensively.

"What about the accountant? Wallace had . . . what's that firm?"

"Blackbourn."

"Oh, yes. Woman named Lippincott. She spent a lot of time out here. She should know something."

"She knows everything," Tillie admitted, hearing the resentment in her tone. "She's the one who told me there was a lease payment." At Mack's sudden frown, Tillie rushed on. "But I didn't stop to think about what effect it might have on the sale. Honest."

The creases in Mack's brow eased slightly. "Considering you're the person Wallace trusted most in this world to take care of things, I believe you."

Tillie thought that she should be the one wondering whether or not to believe Mack Swazee. Still, he wouldn't say he had a receipt for the money if he didn't.

Mack offered a thought. "Ralph Delanoy? Are you getting any help from him in this changeover?"

A sudden twinge of self-pity raised Tillie's voice to a squeak. "Ralph is out of the country. His nephew who works in the law firm was supposed to be a backup for Ralph, but he went skiing on Mt. Hood and broke a leg. He's at a hospital up in Oregon."

Mack cursed under his breath.

Tillie stalled. "Just give me a little time. I'll get our records straightened out." What was she going to do? Ask everyone if they'd happened to find fifty thousand dollars in cash lying around? "Don't worry about the lease payment. Don't worry about anything."

But when Mack left, he did look worried.

Tillie closed her office door and immediately took down the landscape hanging over the wall safe. She had never seen the lease. The conversation with Lynn Lippincott about its terms had taken place the same afternoon Tillie had discovered the insulin needles in the refrigerator. She had neglected to follow up.

The lease was in an unmarked envelope sandwiched between a yellowed warranty on a typewriter and a larger envelope marked *Personnel Notes*.

Tillie smoothed open the multiple sheets of paper. The document seemed to be legitimate. She thought it strange that Wallace would have agreed to a small monthly payment with the huge payment due a few weeks from now. She had to assume that Wallace's signature was authentic as it resembled ones she'd found on the insurance premium payment checks that had never been mailed.

The landlord's signature caught Tillie's attention. She remembered the landlord as being a Mr. Grouchman only because she and Wallace had made private jokes about the name. However, the firm name on the lease was the Grouchman-Richards Company, and a Clayton Richards had signed.

Tillie picked up the phone. "Esther, do you have a file on Mr. Grouchman?"

"The landlord? Sure. Just a minute, I'll get it." She returned shortly. "It's kind of thin. Nothing in it except some old correspondence."

"No copies of leases."

"No. Not now."

"Was there ever?"

"Used to keep them here, but there was a big housecleaning not long ago and I guess those got moved."

"Uncle Wallace cleaned house?"

Esther snorted. "In a matter of speaking. He and Puckatt. I think Lippincott did most of it."

"Any letters from Mr. Grouchman in the file?"

"Old ones. The file isn't exactly on him anymore."

"What do you mean?"

"He's dead. Died a few months ago. Didn't see him around for a long time, not since he merged."

"Merged?"

"Well, in a way. Took in a partner. It's Grouchman-Richards now. You want me to bring the file?"

"I guess not. Thanks." Tillie refolded the lease and put it back in the safe. Where was Ralph Delanoy when she needed him? Where had he been when Wallace signed this lease?

Soon after Mack Swazee left, John Puckatt wandered in, looking fastidious as always in sharply creased trousers and a silk shirt topped by a designer golf jacket.

Tillie was in the front office speaking to Janelle. The young woman had turned out to be so efficient that no additional office help was needed. She and Esther managed well, and Esther seemed to like it that way, although she reminded Tillie often that when things "got to hopping" around there, she would need another person.

After a general greeting, John edged around behind Esther, in a position to read over her shoulder as she transferred information to the computer screen from the copy of a contract spread open on her desk.

"Finally learned to spell *contractual*, I notice." He drew the words out, intending to tease.

Esther glared over her shoulder at him while his attention remained calmly directed to the computer screen.

With a tap of one red fingernail, Esther exited the file. John's perusal switched from the blank screen to her desk, whereupon Esther executed a general swirling of papers that hid the contract and almost every other paper from sight.

"Since you no longer work here, there's no need for you to be concerned about my spelling," she said. "What dragged you in?"

John looked hurt. "I'm missing some personal mail that might have been delivered to this address. Catalogs and magazines. Thought I'd check back in my office for any that might have come."

Esther rejected that reason summarily. "All the mail passes through my desk, and none of it has been for you."

"Come on, Esther, can't I drop in and see old friends? You know, this place was my life for a good number of years."

"Six, to be exact."

John appealed to Janelle. "I'm finding out that it's easier on a person if he breaks old ties somewhat gradually."

"Oh, I know," said Janelle wisely.

Tillie thought that Janelle looked about at the age to have recently broken ties with her stuffed animals.

"Speaking of cutting ties gradually, John, we're all for that," Tillie interjected. "You promised to come back and help us out. We're waiting."

John arranged the pencils on Janelle's desk. "Conflicts. I keep having conflicts."

"We're going through a transition phase, and having you here would make things easier, at least until we get better organized."

"Is the bidding up to date?"

Tillie nodded, although she wasn't positive. "When can I count on you coming in?"

"It'll be soon. Getting many jobs?"

"A couple."

John twisted the diamond ring on his little finger. "Things may pick up for you shortly. Have to expect a little setback with such a major change. Of course, business always slows down this time of year. Want me to look over anything as long as I'm here?" He lowered his voice and rolled his eyes toward Esther. "I notice she's working on a contract."

Esther announced firmly as if John had been consulting her, "No thanks. I can handle it. Operations managers don't have a lot to do with contracts anyway."

John blinked.

Esther added under her breath, "except in some cases."

Braving Esther's wrath, Tillie suggested, "Given the circumstances, maybe it would be good to have our operations manager review the contract."

"Except we don't have one," Esther pointed out, "and the one we did should have caught a certain huge problem on a certain recent contract."

John reared back in surprise, his cheeks puffed with a suppressed retort.

Janelle stared open-mouthed.

Tillie didn't want to air the Olands contract problem in the front office, but John walked over to Esther's desk and accepted her challenge.

"All right, Esther, out with it." His tone was patronizing. " 'Fess up, now, you're still carrying a grudge against me over that stock investment you made a year ago."

"*I* made? At your promise that it would pay back a mint."

"There are no guarantees when it comes to investing in the stock market."

"I suppose not. I suppose somebody can always change the figures, just like the Olands contract."

Tillie cleared her throat loudly but was ignored.

John was dead serious now. "If you're accusing me of doctoring contracts, you'd better be able to prove it."

Esther mumbled something and turned a shoulder to John, suddenly intent on her computer screen.

Austin walked in at that moment.

"I said," John spoke louder, "you'd better be able to prove your accusations."

Tillie sought to stop this exchange before it got completely out of control. "Esther, would you mind going out to the shop and asking Sandoval if he got all the tags he needed today?"

Austin spoke up. "He did. I just talked to him." He turned to John. "Finding it hard to stay away?"

Tillie fumed. Austin was fully aware that she had asked John to come back temporarily.

"On the contrary," John answered. "But I'm trying to arrange my affairs so I can help Tillie over the rough spots."

Austin grinned innocently. "A certain loyalty to the old employer, right?" Austin's hostility could be classed as politely civil.

"Right," John chirped, then ignored everyone but Tillie. "Your uncle and I were friends. I want to do anything I can to preserve this company. In a way, it's his heritage."

Tillie gulped back a lump in her throat at the sentiment. At the same time, she wanted to yell at Puckatt and demand why in the world he was stalling if he wanted to help. She turned in exasperation to the office manager. "Esther, please go out in the shop and check with Sandy." She added for Austin's sake, "Just in case he needs anything else."

Esther pushed her chair away from the desk, leaning back stiff-armed until the chair creaked. She stared at John through half-closed eyes. "If you and the boss got along so well and everything was hunky-dory before your so-called retirement, why was there so much talk of discharging people?"

The remark hit hard. John sputtered.

But before he could retort, Tillie said, "John, come on back to my office." She led the way, stepping smartly past Austin, who jerked open a file cabinet and began studying the folder labels in the top drawer. A crimson flush colored John's face.

When they got inside Tillie's office, John dismissed the entire conversation. "I guess Esther and I act like kids sometimes."

Tillie nodded.

"I should never have advised her on investing money," he said. "I shouldn't try to help people that way. But I felt sorry for her. She doesn't know anything about the stock market. She would have ended up picking an investment by throwing a dart at the stock tables."

"A little like loaning money to a friend, I suppose."

"Yeah. Don't."

"Or doing business with a friend." The image of Mack Swazee sitting in the chair where John Puckatt now sat renewed the cloud of uncertainty that seemed to surround Tillie.

"Not a good idea either," John advised.

Tillie swiveled Wallace's desk chair from side to side. There was a subject she had to address. "Esther raised a fairly nasty matter a few minutes ago. Besides questioning your retirement, I mean."

John played with his diamond ring. "We could always check the personnel records and confirm my retirement."

"No need to do that. Do you know anything about the Olands contract?"

"Should I?"

"There is some irregularity in the dollar amount. Can you shed any light on a special arrangement that my uncle could have made with Olands? Perhaps a discount with the prospect of more business?"

John coughed gently behind one fist. "Nothing that I know of. Esther is right in that contractual arrangements weren't my primary area. As you know, I dealt with getting the job done. Oh, I was privy to the general terms but not the actual paperwork." He quickly added, "Not that I couldn't help you in that respect. That's what I was offering to do out there."

Tillie frowned. No answers here. She wondered how much to tell John. Despite Esther's insinuation that the operations manager had been fired, Tillie was tempted to confide in him, to ask if he knew something of the sale arrangements between Swazee and Wallace. More than anything, she needed a confidant.

John settled into the chair. "I'm glad of the opportunity for this private chat, Tillie. Your situation has been weighing heavily on my mind." He paused for a moment. "I'd like to offer a suggestion, if I may."

"The suggestion box is open."

"Well, I know that this company isn't what it once was. Companies do peak. Not every organization continues to flourish and expand indefinitely."

"Uncle Wallace aimed for slow, steady growth."

"And he achieved it for years. But now things are different. What if the company begins a significant decline?"

It was almost humorous that John spoke of decline as being a future possibility, not a present reality. "That's why I'm anxious to get you back here, John," Tillie said. "It will be temporary, I promise. I can learn from you and take my time hiring a permanent operations manager. And I'll be better equipped to do the hiring."

"Maybe there's a more advantageous course."

"Oh?" Was it her imagination, or did John's silk shirt ripple as his breath quickened?

"Consider selling the company."

Tillie's grip tightened on the arms of Wallace's big chair. John already knew about the pending deal with Mack Swazee.

John continued. "It could be the solution to a lot of problems." He waved vaguely. "Not that you aren't able to handle problems. You can, of course. But difficulties have a way of escalating." He sighed. "Sometimes we have to give so much to gain so little."

"True, but what appears to one person to be a small gain might be quite satisfying to another."

John eyed her intently. "Well, only you can judge whether or not holding on to this company is worthwhile for you personally. Watching it go downhill could be painful."

The last words sounded a warning, but John quickly adjusted his tone to one of encouragement. "I'm sure there are buyers out there who would be extremely interested in a company with a reputation for past quality and honest dealings."

Something kept her from bringing up Swazee's name.

John stood to leave. "I'm just suggesting, mind you. I know Wallace never entertained thoughts of selling, even when he couldn't keep on top of everything."

Perhaps John didn't know about Swazee after all.

"You have to think about your future, and that of Wallace's wife."

John's parting words heaped guilt on Tillie. She didn't want to let go of Kombardee Steel, but it was becoming harder and harder to justify her yearning.

A few minutes later, she was standing by her desk, sorting through a pile of folders, when she heard a polite but indistinguishable exchange between Austin and John out in the hallway. Afterward when Austin joined Tillie, she thought he probably wanted to make himself scarce while John looked for his catalogs. But Austin had something on his mind.

"We don't need Puckatt hanging around here. Things will shape up without his interference."

"His assistance is what I'm hoping for."

Austin smoothed the bandage on his injured hand. "I'm not sure he will be of much assistance."

"You don't care for him any more than Esther, do you?"

"It's not purely personal. I don't think he's reliable."

"I don't remember Uncle Wallace complaining."

Austin used his good hand to roll up the other sleeve. "Reliable was a poor choice of words. Honest, trustworthy, ethical, those might be more appropriate."

Tillie banged a folder on the desk's surface, shaking the contents into place. "Does Esther's inference that Wallace fired John have anything to do with your opinion?"

Austin suddenly unrolled the sleeve he was working on. His motions took on an erratic pattern. "Of course not." His fingers fumbled with the button. "But there could have been good reason."

"Are you suggesting Esther's little jab about changing figures on the Olands contract is valid?"

"I'm not suggesting anything."

"Well, you know what I think? I think Esther's chewing on sour grapes. If John can help us, why not take advantage of his experience?" Only this morning, she and Austin had committed to work together to turn the company around. "Look, I'll check the personnel files and set the record straight. Will that make you feel better?"

Austin's attitude changed dramatically. "No, don't do that. You're right. We'd know if Wallace axed John."

Tillie was startled at the about-face but tried to do her part to resolve the issue. "I'll find out if he was fired. I want it settled."

"It's rather a waste of time to poke around in matters that are behind us, don't you think?" Austin finished the button and shook his sleeve into place.

"I don't understand you. If my uncle fired anybody, I need to know about it."

"Ignore what I said. I'm sorry I raised any objections to the man."

Tillie shook her head. "Let's forget about Puckatt. If he finds time in his busy schedule to do a few days' work, okay. If he doesn't, that's okay too." She held out her hand. "We can do the job ourselves. Agreed?"

Austin's good hand closed over hers. "Agreed." The bandaged one clamped on top of that.

She teased, "Your hand can't be too badly hurt."

He grinned as she waited for him to release her hand. Every second that he didn't, an unexpected camaraderie grew between them. His warmth, exciting and promising, became a current that she was loathe to break, one that seemed to pull her closer and closer to him. She wanted to follow it, to flow with it.

She looked into his blue eyes, searching for old passions that might wait beneath those heavy blond lashes. The pressure of his grip began to hurt Tillie's hand. His lips moved wordlessly. She followed her emotions, leaning toward him with her eyes closed and her lips parted.

Abruptly, Austin flung her hand from his and stepped back from her. His harsh voice shattered the fragile moment. "We can get this company back on its feet. I'll stay with it until we do."

Austin strode through the door, slamming it shut behind him.

He'd felt the intensity of their emotions as strongly as she. Tillie turned sadly to the window and stared at the hills in the distance. Once, wildly in love, she'd thought she understood Austin Neff. She had been sure she could mold this handsome man into her perfect Christian husband. Apparently, she still didn't understand him.

Reluctant to rehire John Puckatt, he nonetheless didn't seem to agree or care that John was fired. Tillie herself couldn't remember the last time Wallace had fired an employee. But then the final days of Wallace's life had not been ordinary ones.

twelve

Tillie decided to telephone Lynn Lippincott. After a short exchange of pleasantries, Tillie asked, "How well do you know my landlord?"

Lynn replied succinctly, "I've met Clayton Richards."

Tillie was not in the mood for playing games. "What are my chances of postponing the lump sum payment on the lease?"

The silence at the other end of the line lasted long enough to make Tillie squirm. Then Lynn answered, "It's getting close to the due date. That doesn't help. Puts him in control."

Tillie knew Lynn Lippincott wouldn't like the idea of another person being in control of anything with which she was connected. Tillie tried pleading her case. "We've been tenants here for many years."

"I doubt sentiment will sway Richards."

"He would have to locate another tenant, and there would be some down time during the changeover. Plus, we have made a few improvements." Tillie was almost embarrassed to stretch the truth that far, considering the current deplorable condition of the yard.

Lynn ignored the arguments. "It's possible Richards might be willing to renegotiate the lease. He seems reasonable."

Tillie was dubious. "A simple postponement would do me more good. I'm not ready for a new lease." She was still reeling under the effects of the prior negotiation with Wallace.

"Would you like me to contact him? As your accountant?"

Tillie was reluctant, but perhaps using a third party would strengthen her bargaining position. "Please do.

Set up a meeting."

"I'll have to give him a reason."

"Don't suggest I can't, er, won't make the payment. Tell him I'm interested in discussing some items about our agreement."

"Yes. Renegotiating. I'll call you."

Tillie hung up with a sigh. She was going to have to stop letting that woman get under her skin. She leaned back in the desk chair and closed her eyes. Several checks had come in the day's mail, enough to meet payroll, so they were staying afloat as far as current payables. But she still owed fifty thousand dollars. In a manner of speaking, she owed it twice. She didn't know how legitimate or binding Mack Swazee's verbal agreement with Wallace was, but if he could prove he'd advanced Wallace the fifty thousand, she'd have to return it to him if she didn't sell. If she did sell, the proceeds would be that much less. In either case, she had to satisfy the landlord who would claim his fifty thousand.

There seemed to be no record of the proposed sale anywhere. Tillie hesitated to tell anyone else, even Austin. She'd quizzed him, but was afraid to admit to him that she couldn't find such a huge sum or even tell him of having a buyer.

Was it because, deep in the recesses of her mind, she entertained unpleasant thoughts that Austin might know more than he appeared about this whole situation? Perhaps once he had known of a willing buyer, he'd consummated the sale, and would be turning his mother's share over to her. Soon he would go running back to his old digs.

Wearily, Tillie pulled out Wallace's ledger. She'd gone over it several times to no avail. She thumbed from back to front through pages labeled *Payables* covering the previous few months. She switched to the *Receivables* and read carefully, beginning with the most recent page. She smiled at one entry,

Psalm 121. The Bible was such a natural part of Wallace's life. She set aside the ledger and picked up his Bible.

It seemed to fall open to Matthew, but she herself had turned to the fifth chapter in that book many times the past days. Knowing the words by heart, she repeated the sixteenth verse, "Let your light so shine before men, that they may see your good works, and glorify your Father which is in heaven."

Wallace lived that mandate from Jesus Christ. Maybe that was why he patiently tolerated the coarseness, the immorality, the childish behavior of some employees. He tolerated, but he did not condone. He hoped his kindness to them would result in their recognizing his own source of strength. It was one thing to tell them of it, another to show that the Lord can light lives with the inner peace of salvation.

Tillie closed the Bible and stroked its worn edges. *Lord,* she prayed silently, *let me glorify You as I try to hold this company together. Let me treat my coworkers as Your representative. I know I can never replace Uncle Wallace, but please help me be a worthy substitute.*

After a while, Tillie put away the Bible and opened the cover of the big checkbook. She flipped slowly through the left margin of stubs, three to a page, that remained after checks had been written and torn out.

She pulled from the pocket in the cover the copies of monthly financial statements with Wallace's notes. There was the deeply imbedded question mark he had traced over and over when studying the discrepancy in the inventory figures. At least one mystery had been unraveled with the discovery of Pierre and Judd selling new reinforcing rods as scrap.

As the pages with his notes flipped by, she reversed her action and removed a sheet with scribbled figures at the bottom. She adjusted the paper in the light. Yes, just as she had once decided, the numerals scrawled here and boxed in with heavy lines indicated a dollar figure, fifty thousand. There was the word she had interpreted as a man's name, *Ernest*. But it wasn't a man's name. Looking closely, she could see the letter *a* squeezed in the cluster of letters, followed by the words, *to be pd*.

Tillie's heart seemed to pause and then jump ahead. Here, in Wallace's own handwriting, was evidence that the earnest money had been expected. Mack Swazee was telling the truth, at least up to this point. But that didn't prove Wallace had received any money, she reminded herself. There was no record of a bank deposit. Only Ralph Delanoy could say whether or not she was legally obligated to carry out the sale, even if the deposit had been paid.

There was still the problem of the money owed to Grouchman-Richards.

If Swazee's payment were hidden in this office, she should have found it by now. In the process, she managed to remove some of the clutter. A spot had been found for the little refrigerator behind her chair, although she never used it. She swiveled the chair and eyed the brown cube. With a dive, she dropped to the floor and jerked open the door. On her knees, she examined every inch of its tiny interior. She found nothing inside, outside, or underneath it.

Feeling slightly neurotic, she stood up. Wallace was not one to hide money in odd places anyway. He used banks, and she'd checked the bank statements ad nauseam. She needed some fresh air. She'd get a cup of coffee and visit a few minutes with Janelle and Esther. After all, she knew absolutely nothing about Janelle except that she was a terrific worker.

Tillie flung open her office door, but had to turn back at the telephone's ring. She leaned over the desk and picked up the receiver.

It was Lynn Lippincott. "I've arranged a meeting with Clayton Richards."

"Already?"

"We will meet you at your office tonight at seven."

Tillie fiddled with the phone cord, uneasy at being here at night. "What about tomorrow morning or Monday?"

"Tomorrow is Saturday and Richards has weekend plans. I had to talk fast to persuade him to come at all. Monday, I'm flying back east for a meeting. After that. . . ." She finished ominously. "Time is running out."

Tillie bit her lip in concentration. "What about meeting at a restaurant?"

"I did suggest it, but he's funny about that. Says if he is dealing on a property, that's where the dealing should take place. Rather quaint, don't you think?"

"Eccentric, I'd say." Tillie didn't have much choice. A noise through the open doorway caught her attention. She leaned to where she could see some of the hall and finished the conversation. "I will be at the office at seven tonight. If I get here first, I'll leave the small gate unlocked for you."

"Good."

Tillie replaced the receiver and went to the door. John Puckatt was the only person in sight. He was coming her way with a smile on his face.

"Found something of mine." He waved a dog-eared magazine with a bar graph prominent in the cover design.

He drove away in his Porsche while Tillie was still pouring her coffee. She'd lost interest in visiting with Janelle after all. She was too worried about the outcome of tonight's meeting. Esther came in from the shop, made a stop somewhere in the back office, and then settled herself at her desk.

Tillie told her, "Try and locate Austin for me."

"He left a while ago. Said he had personal business. Won't be back until late, maybe not at all."

"Did he say where?"

"No. But funny thing, he took his tool belt. At least, it's not on the peg by his door."

"Try to get him on the car phone. I need to talk to him."

Esther didn't reach Austin.

Tillie said, "If he calls in, tell him it's important."

She went back to the office and paced a few turns in the throes of indecision. Her personal savings were mostly tied up in the inventory she was collecting for her shop. She sighed. So far, she'd avoided raiding the one place she could get a big chunk of money. Now she had no choice.

Tillie picked up the phone and dialed Dee. She'd feel her aunt out. She knew saving the business was important to Dee, but was it critical enough to borrow temporarily from the equity in the house? Furthermore, Tillie hoped Dee would know Austin's whereabouts. She counted on his presence here this evening to ease the intimidating prospect of facing her accountant *and* her landlord.

After a few minutes of idle talk at Dee's kitchen table over iced tea, Dee abruptly got up and dumped her tea down the sink.

"Tillie, as long as you're here. . . ." Dee darted from the room and came back with a disorderly armload of papers and her checkbook.

Dee was notorious for not being able to reconcile her bank statements. "Need a fresh eye on the checkbook?" Tillie asked.

"Do you mind? I'd appreciate it so."

Tillie waded through two monthly statements without trouble, trying to explain each step as she went. She kept watch on the driveway, hoping that Austin would show up.

"You're so good at this," Dee said. "I think I understand."

Tillie knew Dee could understand, but somehow the woman's attention flitted on to the next item or to a bit of news that had to be shared right that minute. Sometimes Dee wandered into memories so poignant that it became difficult for Tillie to see the columns of figures for the tears that gathered in her eyes. She finished as quickly as she could, stopping once to call the office and see if Austin had arrived or telephoned.

As Tillie folded the reconciled statements and replaced them in their envelopes with the canceled checks, Dee shoved a small stack of opened mail toward Tillie. The top one bore the gas company logo.

"These are bills." Her hands fluttered over the envelopes. "I can pay them now that I'm sure the bank balance agrees with my balance. That's a good feeling."

"It sure is." Tillie knew that Dee was perfectly capable of writing checks for utility bills.

"It's not these that bother me," Dee said. She fanned the envelopes over the tabletop until she found the one she wanted and handed it to Tillie. "I don't understand this. They are talking about such a large amount."

Tillie opened the envelope. Baffled, she studied a letter from a local bank concerning a home equity loan. With a sinking feeling, she admitted, "I don't understand it either. Did you call the bank?"

Dee looked slightly offended. "Of course. They say Wallace took money from our equity in this house. I tried to tell them the house was paid for. Wallace said a long time ago that there wasn't any mortgage. I own this house free and clear."

A shiver rippled over Tillie's arms and her throat tightened. She shouldn't have drunk the iced tea so quickly. "Did Uncle Wallace tell you he was borrowing from the equity? Did he talk about needing money?"

Dee cocked her head thoughtfully. "Nothing unusual. I mean, a person always needs money. It takes a lot to run a company. He said some of the contractors we did work for were slow about paying, and our company had its own bills to pay."

Tillie stared at the page. Worrying about asking Dee to borrow on the house had been futile. Much of that precious last reserve had been exhausted by Wallace even before Tillie thought of using it—probably to pay pressing costs like forklift repairs or workers' compensation insurance. If this were no mistake, Dee's home no longer belonged to her, as she said, free and clear.

Arriving back at Kombardee Steel, Tillie found there had been no word from Austin. In her office, she removed the landscape picture to expose the wall safe and took out the lease, intending to review it thoroughly before her meeting.

As she removed the lease, she uncovered a large envelope marked in Wallace's scrawl, *Personnel Notes*.

The tiff she'd had with Austin over whether or not Puckatt was fired loomed in her mind. Beset by curiosity, she snatched up the personnel envelope and carried it with the lease to the desk.

Wallace had kept files too private to be in the front office general files in a desk drawer. These were mostly personnel files and Tillie had already examined them. There had been none on John, but Tillie assumed what existed had been removed from the active files when he retired. There wasn't one on Austin either, but then Wallace's stepson was an unusual case.

The contents of the large personnel envelope were rather sparse, containing a few forms and a handwritten list of salaries of key employees, including Wallace's own. Puckatt's was there and Esther's, with a future date and a higher figure jotted beside her name, evidently a planned raise. Nothing was listed for Austin. She recalled that he wasn't in the computer either. Maybe Austin never took a salary.

She recognized the forms as the pink copies of a standard three-part form used in listing changes in status for personnel. The first was a raise for Puckatt given over a year before. Then came a change in title for one of the detailers. Both were clearly written in Wallace's old, steady handwriting.

The next pink form was hard to read. The pressure put on the original must have been erratic, but Tillie saw that the name at the top was Austin Neff. As she tried to decipher the notations, a lump rose in her throat at the date. Wallace had made out this form on the day of his death. A box labeled *Reason* was filled in, the words sprawling over the lines. Tillie studied them intently, finally reading the phrase, *Disregards authority.* Her eyes darted to a group of tiny boxes on the upper right corner. One box was checked, the mark so heavy it nearly obliterated the little square. She gasped as she read the fine print opposite. This form had been used to discharge an employee. Mystified, she returned to the name at the top of the form. No, Wallace had not fired John Puckatt. He had fired his own stepson.

thirteen

Tillie jammed the contents back into the *Personnel Notes* envelope and returned it to the safe. What had Austin done to warrant Wallace's drastic action? Austin didn't even seem to be taking a salary.

She spread her uncle's ledger, checkbook, and all the recent statements out on the desk. There had to be a way to evaluate at least the financial situation. Could she keep the company?

Tillie found it hard to accept that Swazee's earnest money had been nickel and dimed away. Kombardee's meager bank balance would satisfy most of the outstanding payables, but the fifty thousand lease payment would have to be paid from the planned proceeds of the sale. Now an additional debt must be deducted from the proceeds, the amount due on Dee's house. The missing down payment and the lease payment, plus the mortgage balance, totaled a sizeable sum. Even with Tillie not reaping a cent, Dee's nest egg was shrinking by the minute. Selling wasn't an entirely satisfactory solution, although it might be the only one.

On the other hand, if she kept the company, as was becoming more and more important to her, and business picked up dramatically, she could do a creative balancing act with the creditors, do something about the lease payment, and. . . . Tillie ticked off the insurmountable *ifs*. She turned for another look at the balance written on the last stub in the open checkbook, as if it would have changed in the past few minutes. She needed Austin to help her do more than survive, and in one of his final acts on this earth, her uncle had fired Austin. She desperately needed to know why.

A knock on the office door brought her up short. "Yes?"

Esther stepped in, obviously a temporary stop on her way out the door. "You remember I'm leaving early this afternoon?"

Tillie didn't, but she mumbled, "Okay, Esther. Go when you need to."

"It's the weekend. I'll close up everything out there. Janelle is gone." Esther spared a moment to look apologetic. "I'll drop the mail at the post office."

"Thanks."

Esther started to pull the door closed, but paused to scrutinize Tillie. "Anything wrong?"

Tillie brightened. "No. Everything's fine."

"That Puckatt can be a pill. I hope he didn't upset you, or give you any advice." Esther toyed with a ringlet, winding the hair around one finger. "Don't worry. Have a good weekend."

After Esther closed the door, Tillie paced the room. She was desperate enough to listen to any advice, even Puckatt's. He'd said sell. But the plain fact was she didn't want to.

Suddenly from the hallway she heard Austin speaking to a detailer. Her own throat went dry. She wanted to see him and yet she didn't. She marched over and sat down in the president's chair. While she was still deciding on the best way to face the man she loved, he rapped on the door and opened it in one motion.

She didn't like the sarcasm she heard in her own voice. "Why don't you come in?"

He gave her an odd look. "Thanks, I will."

She picked up a pencil and put it to work scribbling on a tablet to give her idle hands something to do.

He sat opposite her, watching. "Anything the matter?"

"Why?" she challenged.

"You seem frazzled."

"Frazzled?" Suddenly, the anger and bewilderment surfaced. "Why shouldn't I look frazzled? There's been enough strange things going on around here to make anyone frazzled."

"Oh?"

"You know very well what I mean. Every day brings a new discovery. Contracts altered. Employees stealing inventory. Drug dealing on my property. Not enough revenues to pay the bills. New equipment that we can't afford." She gave him a dark look.

"We've already been over the matter of that blueprint machine."

Her tone turned petulant. "Well, we still can't afford it."

"It's done now. Let's concentrate on getting some new jobs."

"Perhaps our problem lies in not having enough competent personnel."

Austin dismissed the obstacle with a wave of his hand. "Forget about Puckatt. I have a line on a man from another company who would be a great employee. He knows the business. If we can convince him the risk in coming over with us isn't too great, he might consider it."

Tillie leaned back in the chair, her gaze fixed on Austin. "I wasn't thinking particularly of John Puckatt's absence. I was thinking of the usurper to the throne."

"Hey, if you're still unhappy about me using that title, I'm sorry."

Tillie spoke deliberately. "It's not the title. It's the man."

Austin thoughtfully rubbed the back of his hand on his face, pressing his lips against a knuckle. "You're having a problem with me?"

Now that she'd brought up the subject, Tillie didn't know how to proceed. And she didn't want to.

At her silence, he questioned, "I'm not holding up my end? Not hanging around the office enough? Not out on the job sites enough? Not supervising properly? Assuming too much authority?"

"No, no. I need to talk with you about something." Tillie would have felt inadequate holding this conversation with anyone, but she had an overpowering private interest in this man.

Austin backed off a bit. She avoided his eyes by looking at the ceiling. "It's a touchy matter, but I have to get it out in the open. Maybe there's a good explanation."

"About what?"

Her eyes moved down to his sunbleached hair. "I found something in Uncle Wallace's papers that involved you."

Austin's mouth tightened.

She looked him full in the face and continued. "A copy of the company's personnel form shows that you were fired."

Austin's only sign of distress was a slow shifting of his weight in the chair while his gaze on her never wavered.

After an awkward silence, Tillie asked, "What did you do to make your own stepfather fire you?"

"I'd just as soon not discuss it. Your uncle wasn't rational. He would have changed his mind when he cooled down."

"Then he actually did fire you?"

"I suppose."

Tillie was aghast. "You suppose? The copy of the personnel form is over there."

"I've seen it, but it doesn't mean anything."

"You mean you've seen the original. He must have given you the original, your walking papers, as the saying goes."

"You're making too much out of a simple piece of paper dashed off in anger."

Tillie leaned forward. "My uncle got angry enough with you to discharge you. You must have pulled some horrific stunt to rile that gentle man."

"Can't you take my word for it that the whole episode was a mistake, the act of a man lashing out because things weren't going well?"

"No, I can't." Tillie heard her own harsh words and relented slightly. "I mean, can't you explain?"

Austin dropped his head in his hands and rubbed little circles on his forehead with his fingertips. Wearily, he said, "Okay, I admit it. Wallace fired me. And he fired me for deliberately going against his orders. Disregarding authority, he said."

Tillie's voice was a whisper. "What kind of orders?"

"It was my own fault partly, I guess. I kept poking my nose into matters that Wallace considered none of my business—the books, the accounts on the computer, even contracts. Wallace always seemed to come along at the wrong time."

Tillie's mind had stuck on the mention of contracts. "Like the Olands contract?"

Austin waved a vigorous denial with his hands. "Don't pin any contract problems on me. There were too many things constantly going wrong to be a coincidence, and I was just trying to see if I could make sense of it."

"And did you?"

"Unfortunately, I came up with only a few pieces of the puzzle."

They were silent a few moments before Tillie observed, "You haven't explained the part about disregarding authority."

"Remember the field foreman, Earl Jessup," Austin's lips curled in a slight sneer, "the one you liked so because he used to lift you over the rough spots on job sites?"

She remembered mentioning Jessup when they'd come

across his picture in the company photo album.

"It seems that trusted employee had been cheating. Not only did he cheat the company but he cheated the customer."

Tillie opened her mouth to object.

"Hard to believe? Your uncle wouldn't believe it either, and I never got the chance to prove it to him." Austin's bravado slipped a little, but he soon recovered. "Jessup accepted delivery of ungraded steel for a job."

Tillie knew the difference between ungraded stock and graded stock. They always carried a small amount of the ungraded, mostly for drive-in customers who might use it in something like residential patios. Substituting ungraded stock where graded had been contracted for was dangerous, in more ways than one.

She brushed at a smudge of dust on the redwood pencil holder. "Why didn't you tell me about all this? Didn't you think I'd rather hear it from you than find it out by accident?"

"No one else knew about Wallace's tirade. I figured he'd relent. And he would have. . . ."

Tillie remembered something. "You weren't on salary anyway, were you?"

He shook his head. "I came back for one purpose—to protect my mother's interests. I've hung around for the same reason."

Tillie sat back as if Austin had given her a slap.

He noticed her reaction and he rushed to amplify the statement. "Hung around here on this job, I mean. My reasons for staying in Citrus County are entirely different."

Tillie knew it wasn't smart to let her personal feelings intrude on this business matter but she couldn't help it. "Care to elaborate?"

Austin's sharp glance told her that they both recognized the undercurrent of emotion racing through their dialogue. He didn't answer.

She fumbled with the top desk drawer, slid it open, and in an unthinking gesture arranged the assorted pens and pencils so they all pointed the same direction. What she really wanted to do was to get up, fly around the desk, and throw herself into Austin's arms. Instead she decided to take a sensible approach to the problem of Kombardee's future. She'd be blunt, but calmly logical.

"Let's examine this step by step. We both want to protect your mother's interests. Right?"

He nodded.

"The way to do that is to protect the value of the company."

He nodded again but with a noticeable lack of enthusiasm. She tried to make up for it with an emphatic, "Agreed, we have to bring its value up to par and then go from there."

"That's been my main objective all along," he said.

"Mine too." She had never honestly thought he wanted anything for himself out of this. She sat back, took a deep breath, and proceeded. "So, if our objectives are the same, then we need to explore the best way to achieve that single goal."

After a short silence, during which he seemed intent on rubbing out a freckle on the back of his hand, Austin said, "Tillie, I believe we've had this conversation before, at least once."

"But there are a couple of major problems."

"New obstacles? More than the old obvious ones?"

She didn't want to scare him away. She needed him here and she wanted him here. But he had to know. "There is a fifty-thousand-dollar lease payment due on the property. If we don't pay it, we're in big trouble."

Austin sat up with a start, obviously surprised at the news. "Fifty thousand dollars. What kind of lease is that?"

"I think it's legitimate. Lynn Lippincott says Uncle Wallace agreed to it in exchange for better lease terms."

"Lippincott! That cold fish!"

She had to hide her glee at his appraisal of the accountant. "Lynn is willing to try and help me get a postponement. In fact. . . ," she started, trying to tell him of the meeting before he interrupted her.

"A word of warning. Don't put too much trust in Lynn Lippincott."

"How can I not trust my accountant?"

"Just a feeling."

"Well, anyway, I think I can postpone the lease payment, and I'll certainly ask Ralph Delanoy's advice if I don't succeed. If we can get Puckatt back here to coordinate the general operations, that will help." She quickly added, "That is, until we find a replacement for the long haul. Feel free to pursue that man you spoke of."

Austin got to his feet. He spent an extended time inspecting the painting hanging over the safe, as one might study a master-piece in a gallery.

She built her case. "We owe it to ourselves, Austin." Her spirits soared. Verbalizing the attainment of her goal made it seem near, almost real. She and Austin would be business partners, and perhaps that would lead to the kind of partnership her heart yearned for.

He returned to his chair and said, "Tillie, you spoke of the long haul. I have to tell you that I'm more interested in the short-term health of this company. I think we need to whip it into shape and sell it to the first buyer who's willing to pay a decent price."

"Sell?" Tillie's voice quivered. "Wouldn't an ongoing viable company provide the lifelong security your mom needs? I pictured more of a. . . more of a partnership, with both of us holding this place together." She felt herself drowning in feelings of stupidity and embarrassment. "It would be strictly business. I mean, Uncle Wallace did entrust me. He evidently thought I had the good judgment to. . . ." She broke off completely.

"As you must know, Wallace wasn't quite on top of things toward the end. Perhaps, if he'd really considered, or maybe even if he'd been convinced he had another choice, well, he might have made different arrangements."

Anger strengthened Tillie's voice now. "Another choice meaning you as president?"

Austin shrugged. "Granted, that wouldn't have been ideal."

"But preferable?"

He didn't answer.

Tillie's personal emotions played havoc with her common sense, but she plunged on, driven by hurt and disappointment. "You think I'm not fit to run this place. You've never been more wrong. I can negotiate with the landlord. I can restore this company to one Uncle Wallace would be proud of, one that will support Dee for the rest of her life." She pointed a finger at Austin. "You don't care a thing about the legacy of the company. Why, if I wanted to sell, I could do it tomorrow."

His eyebrows raised. "That so?"

"Yes, that's so. Mack Swazee made an offer to Uncle Wallace, a good offer. He even made a down payment."

Austin's face reddened and a vein throbbed in his temple. "Why didn't you say so?"

She turned a shoulder toward him and looked out the window. "Because selling is my decision to make."

Her words lingered in the room until Austin said, "I suppose it is. I hope you make the right decision."

Tillie knew she would cry at any moment. She twisted her hands together, trying to control the waves of misery that washed over her. Austin didn't love her. He couldn't wait to sell and break even this one thin tie that held them together. Maybe he wanted to sell more for that reason than to get his mother established financially. He was anxious to get on with his own life, a life that did not include Tillie Gibson.

She swiveled back to face him. She loved him, but she wanted to hurt him. "Selling isn't so easy. There's a catch to the sale. It seems the agreement was a handshake deal and the money Mack Swazee claims to have paid Uncle Wallace is not accounted for. Fifty thousand. If it doesn't turn up, that will complicate things."

"Don't tell me you've lost that kind of money?"

"*I've* lost it! You were hanging around here when the deal was set up. I came later, remember? I don't know what happened to it or where it is. Did it get deposited in bits and pieces and then frittered away in day-to-day bills? I've searched endlessly for a clue to tell me what happened to it. Maybe you're the one I should be asking." Furiously, she picked up the checkbook and slammed it down. "It's not in our records. Mack claims it was cash. Someone could have helped themselves. Someone might have taken it, convinced they were right to keep it from being squandered."

Austin was on his feet now.

Driven by anger, she barked, "Or maybe to cancel a debt he mistakenly thought. . . ."

His face a pale mask, Austin broke in. "Stop it! You have a buyer. Fine. Sell as soon as you can, but you'd better get the figures right. And if you recruit Puckatt to help you, ask him about the missing money." His fierce gaze transformed his normally warm features into an ice sculpture. "I sure don't have your money. I don't want anything to do with it. Oh, I know my mother probably never invested her inheritance in this company, but she had better not come out on the short end."

He strode to the door and jerked it open. The sound of it slamming behind him rattled the walls, reverberating through Tillie's shattered nerves. She should call him back and tell him of tonight's meeting, but the words would not come.

Tillie leaned wearily against the closed door. Finally, she flicked off the overhead lights and went back to her chair. She sank into it, swiveled toward the window, and stared at the mountains. Their stability, their majesty, their witness to God's power and magnificent handiwork began to soothe her.

Dear Heavenly Father, she prayed, *what a humbling experience to be rebuffed not once but twice by the man I love. I made the mistake years ago of falling in love with him, thinking that my love would change him into a Christian. Now that we hold the same beliefs, what do I do? I try to snare him into working at a job he doesn't want, in a company he doesn't value, with me at the helm.*

She reached for Wallace's Bible and opened it on her lap. The late afternoon light filtering through the window was so poor she had to squint to see the page. She didn't need to read the words now. Just the feel of the book was comforting, and she closed her eyes and continued her prayer.

You know the two things that are always in my prayers. I suppose I already know the answer to my prayer about loving Austin. It's just so hard to accept. I know Your answer to the other will come. Help me to be patient until You show me how to handle the responsibility of this company. Help me to be wise and unselfish. In Jesus' name.

When Tillie opened her eyes, she realized daylight had faded into dusk. A wind had come up, changing the sunny afternoon into the beginnings of a cold, blustery evening. With a start, she saw that there was no sign of a light on outside her office door. She jumped up and hurried to the hallway. A quick survey told her that all the employees had gone.

No wonder, she told herself, *it's past quitting time.* A shudder of apprehension shot through her body. Why hadn't she swallowed her pride and asked Austin not to leave?

Lynn Lippincott and Clayton Richards would be here soon. To leave now and come back in a short time would be senseless. She'd be better off to stay and get some work done while waiting. A check of the doors proved them to be securely locked. Peering outside, she saw the flicker of a newspaper as the wind swept it up and plastered it against the chain-link fence. She noted with some sense of security that the gates were closed. She guessed that Ms. Lippincott would honk when she arrived.

Tillie returned to her own office. She turned on the overhead lights and the desk and table lights but they didn't offer much comfort. She sat down at her desk and opened Wallace's ledger, willing it to claim her full attention. The truth was that she was alone and she was scared.

fourteen

Wallace's handwritten entries in the ledger became less and less legible as the pages neared the date of his death. Endearing, homey comments scribbled here and there tugged at Tillie's heartstrings.

Tonight one especially caught and held her interest. The notation seemed neither to refer to an entry nor to be an added general remark. Instead, this one was written on a line as if to take the place of an entry.

Strange, she mused, that Wallace should write a Bible verse in the ledger opposite a date as if he'd been logging a business transaction. But there it was, *Psalm 121:1*. Something about the hills, if she remembered correctly.

The wind was picking up and with it came rustling, like leaves skittering across hard surfaces or ground squirrels scurrying for shelter. At the unwelcome memory of the snake that had come calling earlier, she drew her feet close and balanced them on the base of the chair.

She pulled a sheet from the checkbook, her own version of Wallace's handwritten summary of the financial statements. Underneath it was his, the one with the puzzling memo about the earnest money.

"Oh, Lord, I need help!" The unbidden words sounded loud in the emptiness of the deserted building. Suddenly in Tillie's mind something clicked. Help—of course—help from the hills. Quickly she reopened the ledger, flipping pages, anxiously bending over the ledger, until she found the Psalm 121:1 entry. Her finger moved across the page to the date. Its date was later than the one scrawled on the sheet where Wallace had written that earnest money was to be paid. It had been written only a few days before Wallace's accident.

She snatched up the Bible and opened it, eagerly thumbing through the Old Testament until she read, "I will lift up mine eyes unto the hills, from whence cometh my help." Psalm 121:1 did promise help from the hills.

Why would Wallace record that Bible verse as a ledger entry unless he meant it to be interpreted that way, interpreted by someone familiar enough with the Bible to recognize the connection? Perhaps it was a kind of code put there to trigger his own memory. Maybe he thought if Tillie herself were studying the ledger, it could be his way of telling her about the money.

Puzzled, she looked through the window where the distant mountain range would be visible had it not been cloaked in darkness. Ill at ease with the black panorama, she quickly drew the blinds. Her watch showed that there was still a little time before Lynn Lippincott and the landlord were due.

She reread Psalm 121:1. Then she read the entire Psalm, taking sweet reassurance in the seventh verse: "The Lord shall preserve thee from all evil: He shall preserve thy soul."

Wallace had loved the mountains; he had, after all, hung the framed painting of the outdoor scene over the wall safe.

Suddenly, it made sense. *The ledger entry clearly directed the reader to the painting of the hills.*

In her excitement, Tillie knocked a stapler from the desk, sending it rattling across the floor. She tried to step over it and succeeded in kicking it into the desk leg, creating yet another jarring interruption. She stopped and drew a deep, uneven breath. In that pause, a third noise sounded outside her immediate office. The wind moaning, she told herself, retrieving the stapler and rushing over to the painting.

She lifted the heavy frame from the wall and propped it on a small table. She examined the oak frame, three inches wide and in need of a good dusting. She whirled the painting around so the brown paper backing faced her. It revealed nothing and appeared to be the original paper.

She tilted the painting and studied its edges intently. The paper backing was stapled to the frame in a rather haphazard manner, as if done carelessly or by a person handicapped by poor eyesight.

Carefully she removed staples, a few at first, then rapidly pulling out the complete row that held the top edge of the brown paper backing to the frame. She couldn't see much behind the covering. She began taking off more staples, working her way down one side until she was able to pull a corner away.

Tillie gave a cry of surprise at the sight beneath the paper. A lightweight, puffy bundle was stapled to the inner edge of the frame, suspended in the cavity between the canvas and the paper backing. Inside what appeared to be a sandwich-sized plastic bag was a bundle of bills. She finished ripping the paper backing off the painting, throwing it to the floor as she gaped in disbelief at the sight of more plastic bags fastened there, each holding currency. She had found the fifty thousand dollars of earnest money.

Tillie looked nervously over her shoulder and stifled her urge to scream out the news. Being there alone at night was unnerving enough, but having custody of this kind of cash made her more jittery than ever.

The low creaking sound she had heard earlier continued, swirling through the building, ebbing and flowing in an almost rhythmical pattern. Such mournful tones gave the office an air of a ship riding out a storm at sea, rather than being simply buffeted by a winter night's wind.

Tillie looked around the office for a temporary depository, wondering why Wallace had chosen to hide the money rather than put it in the bank. The empty refrigerator! Not good, but it would do.

Tillie crammed the bags in large clasp envelopes and stuffed everything inside the small brown cube, unplugging it so the light would not go on if the door were opened. As she did so, she discovered among the plastic bags a white, letter-size Kombardee Steel envelope. Inside on a plain sheet of paper were a few words written in Wallace's unsteady hand: *Deposit half of this in account for Tillie's frilly shop.*

Tears flooded Tillie's eyes. So Wallace had set money aside for her, meaning to open a special account. Knowing her dream, he'd wanted to give her the means to start her shop. With his poor health and failing eyesight, he surely hadn't realized how badly the company's financial condition had deteriorated and that there was barely enough money available to keep afloat. He'd signed the lease, probably not fully understanding it. Still, with all his troubles, he had thought of her.

She shut the refrigerator door and sank wearily into her chair. Why didn't she feel exhilarated at finding this fortune? A few moments ago, she had little control over the future. Now she had the freedom to pay the landlord and keep the company in operation. Alternately, she could sell to Swazee and know that the total net proceeds would more than take care of Dee's needs.

If she kept Kombardee Steel, she might lose everything and Dee and all the employees would come out the losers. Selling Kombardee Steel involved risk of a different kind. With the company safely sold and his mother's financial future secure, Austin would waste no time in cutting ties and getting on with his own life.

As far as her relationship with Austin was concerned, it was clear that she was already a loser. As she tried to convince herself that this was the stark, unvarnished truth, she began to visualize a different picture, one of Austin remaining at Kombardee Steel to help bring the business back to prosperity—if only for his mother's sake. The vision of him at her side loomed ever more tempting in her mind. "He might stay," she said aloud, "he might stay."

Quickly she squelched her wishful thinking. Her head told her, *Don't be a fool. If he doesn't want to be here, you shouldn't want him.*

As Tillie's thoughts seesawed back and forth, she absent-mindedly moved about doing nonessentials. She straightened stacks of papers and blew dust from the computer keys.

Robert Sandoval had told her that Jim and the baby's mother were getting married this weekend. That was encouraging. At the same time she thought of Sandy himself and the others who had been loyal employees, of the field men who took pride in the artistry of their construction work. There was Esther nearing retirement with the heart irregularity that might preclude her getting health insurance elsewhere.

Finally, Tillie punched a number on the telephone. After several rings, she was poised to slam down the receiver. She whispered to herself, "Face it, Tillie, Mack Swazee can better ensure a job for that baby's father than you."

On the ring that would have been his last opportunity, Mack answered.

"That problem about the lease payment is resolved," Tillie told him.

"Glad to hear it." If he were puzzled over a call at this time of night, he didn't show it.

Her voice caught and she cleared her throat. "I need Ralph Delanoy's help to go ahead with the sale. We can get together as soon as he returns."

Obviously pleased, Mack said, "Thanks, Tillie. I know Wallace would be glad that you're finishing a deal he began. He always wanted what was best for his company and his family."

Yes, Tillie thought, *selling Kombardee Steel was best for that new baby, for Dee, for everyone except her.* She must let go and give the company a chance to flourish under a more experienced hand.

She took a long, deep breath, not wanting to let Swazee know of her heartache. Releasing the company meant severing the last opportunity for contact with Austin.

"Incidentally," Mack said, "Given that bizzare arrangement with your landlord, I was doing some checking." Modestly, he explained, "I know a few people around town."

Tillie raised her eyebrows at the understatement.

"It's inconsequential now that you say you've got the lease problem taken care of. But an interesting little quirk showed up."

"What kind of quirk?" Tillie asked.

"No problem with the Grouchman-Richards company, when the old man ran it. Could be no problem now, I don't know. A man in that office is apparently pretty chummy with a friend of yours."

"Oh?"

"Clayton Richards. He attended the last Chamber of Commerce mixer as a guest. Your accountant, Lippincott, was there. On the surface, they didn't seem to be acquainted."

Tillie was about to mention that both were coming over shortly when he continued.

"That may not seem remarkable, but I know her boss, Blackbourn, very well. He was there, too, and getting a kick out of their act—and it was an act—because he happens to know they ski together. Blackbourn owns a condo in the same complex where these two spend their weekends."

Tillie made a face at the incongruous mental picture of Lynn Lippincott cozying up to a man in a mountain retreat.

When Mack received a signal that he had another call, they hung up.

Tillie digested his story, thinking how unlike Mack Swazee to relate that kind of report. He seemed to feel obligated to inform her of the liaison.

She was considering that possibility when a noise startled her again from the direction of the outer office. The wind had increased in velocity, but this sound was not simply the wind blowing.

Cautiously, she flicked off the lights in her office before venturing into the hallway. The outside floods shining in through windows enabled her to progress along the hall with a stealthy step. She paused outside the office Austin had adopted. She was about to flick on the lights when the noise repeated. The creaking whine was not unlike a moving porch swing groaning under the weight of heavy riders.

Caught in growing fear, Tillie listened for more. Just when she thought the spooky sound effects had ceased, the creaking came again, followed by erratic squeaks and scraping. As her fright intensified, she reached for a weapon, her arms sweeping the wall where Austin's tool belt hung, hoping to put her hands on a pair of wire cutters. She couldn't locate the belt.

Then she remembered that afternoon Esther had informed her that both Austin and his belt were gone. Austin had returned and later stormed out of Tillie's office, much too late for him to have returned to the field. The belt must be here. Her hands made another sweep across the wall, this time catching the empty hook.

The mournful song was suddenly joined by a new sound, one

that Tillie could identify. She sighed with relief to hear a car turn into the property. She crept to a side window in the front office. Some of the floodlights that should have been illuminating the main door of the office were apparently out. But from here Tillie could see the chain-link fence and the black car coming through the open gate. It was Lynn Lippincott's Mercedes. For once, Tillie would welcome the woman.

Pondering over the open gate that she remembered as being closed earlier, Tillie delayed moving to turn on the office lights. A faint commotion made her hesitate even longer. From behind her came a little jingle so delicate it could have been the clinking of crystal goblets.

While trying to block out this blood-curdling sound, she quickly began to rethink her approach to the meeting since she had decided to sell. She needed an arrangement that would allow Kombardee Steel to stay in the building until the sale was complete and pay the lump sum on a prorated basis. Surely Clayton Richards wouldn't try to hold her to an unreasonable agreement signed by a deceased person.

Tillie heard muffled voices at the front of the building. Knowing the front door was shrouded in darkness, Tillie hurried to snap on the interior lights.

She flipped the switch and was still blinking at the onslaught of brightness when a woman's scream ripped through the howl of the wind and bridged the distance to where Tillie stood. It was a scream of terror.

Immediately, Tillie clawed at the light switch, restoring the office to semidarkness. She dove for the nearest desk, which was Esther's, and ducked low, putting its wooden hulk between her and the source of whatever caused Lynn Lippincott's panic.

Tillie's mind skipped from one frantic idea to another. Outside, the scream had died, replaced by distraught sobbing. Lynn

Lippincott was crying? Gathering her shredded courage, and satisfied that any danger was outside the building, Tillie scurried to a front window.

A tall man wearing a light-colored jacket stood on the walk leading to the Kombardee office entrance. Huddled close to him was a darkly clad woman, Lynn Lippincott, her head buried in the man's chest. Obviously the man was Clayton Richards. But the emotion both were displaying seemed far removed from what Swazee had hinted at.

Convinced that Lynn had fallen and hurt herself, Tillie turned the office lights back on and dashed toward the door. She pulled it open and rushed outside, only to feel her face and upper body collide firmly with a large, hanging object. The barrier was bulky and heavy enough to offer solid resistance, but it moved under the impact, creaking in protest. She recoiled at first in surprise, then in horror, fighting the onward momentum of her body until she'd managed to propel herself back. The grisly bundle swung back and forth in a short arc, turning and twisting as it went.

fifteen

Tillie shook herself, brushing at her hands and face, trying to shed the repulsive sensations of touching jagged ends of wire, fur, and a thick oozing substance, part and parcel of the gruesome obstacle.

Swinging from the overhang outside the front door, and big enough to fill the width of the open doorway, was a cagelike contraption fashioned of wire mesh. Its pattern of squares was distorted and broken from having been folded into this crude hammock. Squeezed inside was a lifeless-looking gray mass.

Tillie forced her attention on the wire cage long enough to tell that this fiendish chamber held an animal. Judging from its size, and catching sight of a limp paw that dangled through the wire, she concluded that it was a large dog, most likely a German shepherd. A pitiful whimper told her that despite wounds and whatever treatment had been endured, the animal was alive.

Only at that moment did she remember that Austin was to have arranged for a guard dog service, the first dog to be delivered after hours on Friday, today. It must have come while she was shut inside the back office with everyone else gone.

A man's voice roused Tillie from her stunned state.

"Ms. Gibson, are you hurt?"

"I guess I'm okay. Come around to the side," she directed.

Tillie temporarily blocked the horrible sight from her mind by closing the front door. She opened the side entrance and then picked up the telephone.

Lynn Lippincott preceded the man in the light-colored jacket inside. She then introduced the landlord in a word or two, took the telephone from Tillie's trembling hands, and called the police.

Seemingly fully recovered, Lynn said, "What an awful experience for you."

Tillie responded, "And for you. I hope the dog will be all right." She rummaged through Esther's desk top seeking the name of the guard service.

"I was taken by surprise," Lynn explained as coolly as if she were caught in an unpredicted rain shower.

"Shouldn't we do something for the dog?" Tillie wrung her hands helplessly, trying not to look at the closed door.

Clayton Richards cracked the door open and peeked out. "The dog was probably tranquilized but it's beginning to stir. We shouldn't get within striking distance."

Lynn ordered, "Shut that door. Let the police handle it." She took a seat at the spare desk and motioned Richards to sit nearby. She turned to Tillie. "We can proceed. I mentioned to Mr. Richards that you were interested in renegotiating the lease."

The landlord still seemed as nervous as Tillie about a half-dead dog hanging on the other side of the door, but he followed Lynn's lead. "What did you have in mind, Ms. Gibson? Any problems with the facilities?"

Lynn spoke for Tillie. "Let's don't waste words. I believe it's a matter of money. Specifically, the lump sum due this month."

Tillie felt invisible.

A worried frown creased Richards's forehead. "Is there a problem with the payment?"

Again Lynn spoke for Tillie. "No problem. However,

pulling together such a large amount could be a little inconvenient given certain circumstances."

He tapped his fingers on his knee. "Inconvenient?"

They both consulted Tillie. She swallowed. "I wonder how you would feel about a postponement." She'd wait for a little more courage before asking him to prorate the payment.

Richards frowned.

Tillie quickly added, "I'd pay interest, of course."

"How long a postponement did you have in mind?"

"Oh, just a few more weeks."

Richards blinked, as if totally surprised. He seemed to wait for Lynn to respond.

She smoothed her black hair needlessly. "Mr. Richards might consider that if he could be assured the payment would be forthcoming, with reasonable interest, of course." A ghost of a smile played on her red lips.

Tillie watched in fascination as the arbitrator continued the game with the landlord.

Lynn pointed out, "It seems prudent to retain a good tenant, Mr. Richards, unless, of course, you have a better suggestion."

The landlord gave a final tap with his fingers to his knee, stood up, and adjusted his tie. He took a turn or two around the office while the women waited politely. Then he pulled back his jacket and put one hand in his pocket. Standing over Tillie, he suggested, "I may have an out for you."

She answered, "I need a few weeks to get matters under control."

He ignored that as if she were merely saving face. "I make it a practice to keep my eyes open for possible business opportunities. When one comes along, I don't mind adding to my investment portfolio, even if the immediate potential is doubtful." He stroked his chin like a thoughtful professor, looking older than what he probably was, in his early forties. "Yes, my investment policy leans toward long-term growth. We might be able to arrive at an agreement that would benefit both of us."

Tillie was mystified that no one believed her. "As I said, I need a postponement for a couple of months at the most." She didn't want to reveal more than that. This conversation was growing more disturbing by the minute.

Lynn asked the landlord, "What kind of agreement?"

"Ms. Gibson might be open to being relieved of so much responsibility." He spread his hands to include everything in sight. "Not that she can't handle the affairs of this company in a perfectly capable manner. On the contrary, I'm sure she can. But the steel business is not a glamorous occupation."

Clayton Richards wanted to buy her out, and he would make an offer if she gave him half a chance.

Lynn Lippincott provided the opportunity. "Are you saying you might be willing to invest in Kombardee Steel?"

He nodded. "A substantial investment."

Tillie sensed a new urgency, or at least an increased tension between her visitors, possibly because she wasn't rushing to accept whatever crumbs the landlord might be dropping. Little as she cared for Lynn Lippincott, Tillie preferred her crisp, sharp manner to Clayton Richards's impenetrable façade. She told the landlord, "I'll have to think about what you say. Tonight has been terribly unnerving."

"Of course, but we mustn't sit on this too long. I'll call you first thing Monday morning."

She stalked to the side window. "Where are those police? I'll try to locate Austin."

"I don't see how he can help matters," Lynn said quickly.

Tillie had her doubts, too, considering their parting a few hours before. She didn't know where he was anyway. "He should be told about that problem outside." She motioned toward the door and cringed thinking of the pitiful sight on the other side. "He could deal with the police." She returned to the chair at Esther's desk.

Lynn frowned. "Why not call Puckatt? He was your uncle's operations manager. Your uncle trusted him."

The inference was clearly that Wallace did not trust Austin.

The accountant added, "If I may suggest, you might be better off handling matters yourself, rather than relying on a man new to the business, just because he's the widow's relative."

Shocked, Tillie reacted strongly. "Austin is honest. He wouldn't cheat me."

Clayton Richards had returned to his chair by the spare desk. He stretched his legs out and crossed his ankles as if he'd finished his part in this drama. He looked away when Tillie glanced his direction. He didn't know Austin and therefore couldn't be expected to voice an opinion.

Lynn Lippincott, however, was no neutral observer. "It may be a matter of misguided intentions—a desire to gain control, for what he considers good reason. I hesitate to say this, but I feel obligated, for your uncle's sake." She unsnapped her briefcase and snapped it again. "I think you should know that your uncle fired his stepson."

Not wanting to confirm the truth of that statement, Tillie pretended she hadn't heard Lynn's last remark and created a commotion by jumping up, sending the chair rolling back. "The phone number of that guard service may be on Austin's desk. Excuse me a minute."

Feeling less intimidated when out of their sight, Tillie

stepped smartly along the hall. As she approached Austin's office, her attention was snagged by a vague notion that something was awry. Although nothing in his office appeared irregular, as she was checking his card file for the guard service number that notion popped into focus. She stepped back out to the hall. There on the wall, hanging on the hook right outside Austin's office, was Austin's tool belt.

Wondering if she'd simply bypassed it in the dark, she mentally repeated her actions. She'd run her hands all over that wall. She couldn't have missed the belt. Although it wasn't outfitted with as much paraphernalia as the field men hung on theirs, it was still a wide swath of leather with a large buckle. The belt held a spool of wire encased in a thick metal cylinder and contained pouches designed for two pairs of wire cutters.

Tillie stared in consternation at one pair of cutters. The handles were bright and shiny but the pouch where they had been inserted bore a red tinge. Gingerly, she gave a little tug. The leather grabbed and then released the cutters from the pouch. As they slipped out, the remainder of the belt vibrated with a soft jingling sound. To Tillie's horror, the pointed end of the cutters dangling from her hands was stained dark red, the color of blood.

She shuddered and jammed the tool back into its pouch. This belt had been hung in Austin's place. The person wearing that belt had used the tools to encase the tranquilized guard dog.

Could Lynn Lippincott be right? Was Austin's interest in this business so consuming that he would perform a despicable act to frighten her away so he could run the place as he pleased?

Feeling thoroughly sick, Tillie tried to compose herself.

She walked back to the front office empty-handed. If Lippincott and Richards noticed her agitation, any remark they might have made was forestalled by the sound of a car arriving out front.

John Puckatt, in his customary athletic style, sprinted around the building and bounded into the front office from the back door. "What is going on here? I was driving by and saw the lights. Then, I saw. . . ." He stopped and looked at the visitors as if their presence was more of a shock than the harnessed animal hanging outside the door.

Tillie cried, "John, I'm glad you're here. You can talk to the police."

"About time," Lynn remarked, as a patrol car pulled up.

"Who called the police?" John snapped.

"I did," Lynn shot back. "What did you expect?"

John lost some of his argumentative tone and grumbled, "If you call the police for every little thing, they won't be in a hurry to come when you really need them."

Astounded, Tillie said, "Every little thing?" Something about John looked different but she couldn't put her finger on it.

Lynn growled, "John, this is Clayton Richards, Kombardee's landlord."

Although Tillie was upset at John's unfeeling attitude, she thought the accountant showed an inordinate amount of distress with John.

John repeated dumbly, "Landlord?" His eyes darted from person to person almost in a momentary panic before he regained his usual poise. "I'm John Puckatt. I retired from Kombardee recently."

The conversation was halted by yet another arrival. Austin's Explorer roared through the gate and stopped, its driver barely aiming at a parking space. Austin jumped out and ran to one of the officers.

John looked relieved. "Austin is here. I'll be on my way."

But Austin met him at the door. "Don't leave. The police want to get the story on that atrocity." He strode to where Tillie sat limply at Esther's desk. "What on earth do you mean by being out here at night? I found out from Mom that you were supposed to meet these two. Why didn't you tell me?"

Tillie retorted in a hoarse whisper, not meant for the others, "When you stormed out this afternoon, you weren't in the mood to hear me."

"Don't give me that."

"Besides, it got dark and everyone left without my noticing."

"Why didn't you call somebody when you found you were alone? How did you expect to handle the guard dog in the yard?"

"I forgot all about it until I opened the door and. . . ." She buried her face in her hands to shut out the memory.

Austin groaned. "The gate should have been locked. How did these people get in?"

"I don't know." Tillie looked at him in desperation. "All I know is that earlier the gate was shut, I forgot about the dog, and then the gate was open, and I heard noises, and when Lynn and Richards came, Lynn screamed, and I ran outside and. . . ."

Her account trailed off again as she lost her concentration, sidetracked by Austin. His right hand was newly bandaged. The dressing was spotless and larger than the one he'd had earlier.

He answered her unspoken question. "It got to bothering me so I went back to the emergency center. They changed the dressing."

Tillie hated the suspicions going through her mind. "This morning you said it was nothing. Did you injure it again?" Her tone sounded as pointed as the bloody wire cutters hanging in Austin's tool belt.

Tillie couldn't read his reaction, but his blue eyes narrowed beneath his heavy brows and he said nothing.

The police worked rapidly. The animal control people seemed to think the dog would survive. There were surprisingly few questions. Austin talked to the guard dog service by telephone, and soon only the five people connected with Kombardee Steel remained.

Tillie didn't want any more discussion on the lease. She just wanted to go home.

John started for the door but Austin stepped in his way. "As long as we're all here, I want to bring up a few matters." Austin's manner dared anyone to object.

Lynn was perched on the corner of the spare desk. "We came for a business appointment with Tillie. I don't have time for anything else."

Austin glared at her. "Make time."

He pulled an envelope from his jacket pocket. From it he took a folded document of several sheets familiar to Tillie as a copy of their standard contract form. He shook it open and marched around the room, holding it for each person to examine.

The name typed in the top identified this as a contract with Olands. Tillie knew of only one recent contract with them, one she'd rather not see again.

Lynn got up and reached for her briefcase, as if defying Austin's order to stay.

Austin pushed the contract in her face. "I had a rather

intense conversation with Olands today," he told her. "I promised not to pursue the matter, and the president of Olands agreed to let me have this copy of the contract. It is not the copy we have in our file, nor the copy they have in their file, the copies both he and Wallace signed. This is a copy of the contract as it was originally filled out—an unchanged copy—showing that the contract was for fifty-five thousand, not for twenty-two thousand less."

Lynn looked bored but sat back down. Richards played with a telephone message pad. John fidgeted on the edge of his chair.

Austin continued. "As we all know, someone changed the contract, either before or after Wallace signed it. It doesn't matter which. It's still theft."

Richards opened his mouth, plainly objecting to being included, but didn't say anything.

Tillie was having difficulty keeping her mind off Austin's right hand. The new dressing was larger than this morning's. Fresh gauze seemed to have been wrapped over the old. For a moment, she wondered whether removing the new wrappings would reveal stains that weren't on the old bandage before tonight.

"What matters," Austin continued, "is that this is just one in a series of problems that plagued this company and its owner for the past few months. Tonight's episode is no exception."

This time Lynn snatched up her briefcase. "Come on, Mr. Richards. This is an internal issue that doesn't concern us."

"I'd advise you not to leave," Austin threatened. "There are serious matters to be settled." He turned to Tillie. "I finally found out why we can't seem to generate enough money to pay our bills, even when we have the jobs to do it. A dummy account has been set up. It bills the company for bogus amounts. Checks are written to pay the dummy invoices and the money goes right out the door."

"Be careful what you insinuate," Lynn threatened. "I audit the finances of this company on a regular basis. Absolutely nothing illegal goes on."

"What would you call the sizeable account with the generic name of General Accounting?"

Lynn's face paled. "That's an account set up to receive payables. A sort of holding account. Every penny in it is legitimate."

"A holding account to hold the monies out of reach."

Tillie demanded, "She's been stealing from us?"

"In a way," Austin answered. "She's too smart to commit extortion. She simply hid the money so the company would drop deeper and deeper into debt. If her tinkering were discovered, the funds would be there—and still are—in that secret reservoir and she could chalk it up to an accounting error."

For the first time since his fiery entrance, Austin's determination faded a bit. He dropped the contract in front of Tillie and sank into the chair across from her. Wearily, he confessed, "I just don't know the reason behind all of it. I only know that she took advantage of Wallace's deteriorating health to nearly destroy a good business."

Suddenly, Tillie remembered Mack Swazee's story. "I know the reason," she cried. "The lease Uncle Wallace signed requires that fifty thousand dollars be paid this month or Kombardee has to get out immediately. Uncle Wallace didn't understand that." She pointed to Richards and Lynn. "These two work together. Richards tricked Wallace with an outlandish lease. She's been running down the business so Wallace wouldn't have money to make the lump sum payment. The friendly landlord could then offer to take the company off Wallace's hands. Probably for pennies. Just the kind of offer he was trying to make to me tonight." She continued unflinchingly. "An accountant to bleed the company dry. A landlord to step in and take it over." She glared at Clayton Richards. "Stealing from a blind man!"

John threw up his hands. "This is your problem. I don't even work here."

"But you did," Austin corrected, "and I think your handiwork was in it all the way."

John cowered, polishing the top of one shoe by rubbing it against a pant leg, a familiar habit of his.

Lynn was on her feet. "There has been not one iota of wrongdoing. Do you think I would be stupid enough to pull any illegal moves? Kombardee isn't my only account. I have a reputation to protect."

Richards joined her. "That lease will stand up in any court."

Lynn Lippincott seemed to enjoy the fray as she proceeded to flaunt her accomplishments. "Aggressive business methods. That's all. No one can say otherwise."

Tillie was outraged. "Is that what you call it? How many others have you two swindled? How can you stand there and claim to be innocent?" She shook her finger at the accountant. "Your own boss knows you two are a team."

The stab hit home.

"Don't think you can just walk away from all this. Mr. Blackbourn knows about your love nest. When he hears about how you're using his firm as a vehicle for your scheme. . . ."

Richards's eyes widened and he began to breathe heavily. Lynn chewed at her red lipstick.

Austin himself seemed slightly surprised but he promised

more dire consequences. "Perhaps you'll see the seriousness of your so-called aggressive business practices when we file charges for harassment. I seem to recall a rattler let loose in the building. Then we have cruelty to animals."

"Don't be ridiculous," Lynn snapped.

Tillie wondered how much Austin was guessing. She added, "What about intercepting insurance premium payments? Interfering with the mail?"

Lynn sputtered with anger, "Ask your retired operations manager."

At this, John hissed toward the accountant, "Don't blame me. Whatever I did was to help you, and it wasn't anything illegal."

Austin whirled toward Puckatt. "Yes, I thought it was you."

"I never hurt anyone. Lippincott promised me a cut if I'd help things along by planting a few problems here and there. Just disruptions, nothing serious." John fiddled with his thick, wavy hair. "A sort of supplemental retirement in exchange for stirring things up a bit. But you can't prove anything."

"Maybe not," Austin said, "but I see enough right now to convince me that you're the fiend that tortured that poor dog."

John sidestepped toward the back, excitedly pointing the way. "Tillie, go take a look at Austin's tool belt. I noticed blood on it as I came in. I didn't want to cause any more problems for you by reporting it to the police. Austin is the one who strung up that poor dog."

Tillie spoke to John, but her eyes were clearly on Austin. "I don't have to inspect the belt. I already know there's blood on it. I don't understand how it got there, but I know that Austin wouldn't harm a dog." She added softly, speaking only to Austin, "Or me."

Austin gave Tillie such an intensely personal gaze that the

circumstances surrounding them paled momentarily.

With a curt, "Get out of here," Austin dismissed the others.

Lynn walked regally to the door with Richards in tow. As John Puckatt edged toward the back, Austin called to him, "By the front door, John, where I can see you. You'd better use cold water on that jacket. Hot water sets blood."

John left, still claiming, "You're crazy. That's a stain from my golf bag."

Tillie shivered from relief and excitement. Puckatt seemed different tonight because his designer golf jacket was rumpled and dirty. As he slipped out the door, she saw the long red smudge smeared across the lower edge. He'd used Austin's tool belt and then sneaked in and replaced it. He'd opened the gates, too, not knowing that Lynn and Clayton Richards would arrive.

Tillie remembered making the appointment with Lynn on the phone. Her office door had been open. John had overheard that she would be here and had planned this to frighten her. This was another of his disruptions to push Tillie into selling out for whatever paltry sum the landlord would offer. He was aware of the guard dog arrangements, but he didn't know that his cohorts would be the beneficiaries of his despicable tactics.

Tillie wilted with exhaustion. She slumped in Esther's chair, trying to absorb what had happened. Now that they were alone, she should tell Austin about her decision concerning Swazee.

"All this doesn't change one certain matter," she began.

He perched on the outer corner of the desk.

"I made a difficult decision tonight." She hoped she could get through this. How tempting it was to throw herself into Austin's arms and beg him to stay with her, to help her keep the company, to try again for the love they once had.

She told him of finding the money inside the painting, breaking down only when she related how Wallace had designated half of it for her "frilly shop."

"Poor guy," Austin reacted. "No wonder he got confused. He probably wanted that much cash from Swazee because the specter of that lease payment in that same amount haunted him, even though he seemed unsure about it. I get furious when I think of that woman pushing papers around for him to sign, with him nearly blind."

They were both silent for a while. Then he asked, "Well, what is this big decision you've made?"

"I called Mack Swazee. I'll pay whatever Ralph Delanoy says I owe on the lease and then proceed with the sale. There will be enough to settle everything and still take care of your mom."

Austin studied her carefully. "You don't want to sell, do you?"

Not trusting herself to speak, she shook her head.

Austin moved around to her side of the desk. "I'm proud of you. You're doing what's best for your uncle's company."

She could barely contain the sobs. "But not for me."

"Still looking for a partnership?"

Suddenly, Tillie felt she couldn't take any more hurt tonight. "Sorry. I'm not up to verbal sparring or any probing into my personal life. I'm not even up to holding this conversation. I'm going home."

She stalked back to her office, stepping wide around the incriminating tool belt. Tillie scooped the bills from the refrigerator into a briefcase. She grabbed her purse and walked back to the front office, turning off lights as she went.

Austin said, "Be back in a minute. I should check outside.

Wait for me."

She watched him head toward the shop.

The phone rang. A professional-sounding voice said, "This is Anna at the emergency center calling for Austin Neff."

Tillie replied, "He stepped out for a few minutes. Can he call you?"

The woman thought a moment. "Just tell him that he left his insurance card here this evening when he was in to have his hand checked."

When Austin returned, Tillie said, "A call came for you from the emergency center."

He waited, watching her.

"You left your insurance card there this evening."

A sparkle danced in his blue eyes. "I'll pick it up tomorrow," he said, still studying her.

She started toward the door. "I'd better go."

Austin crossed the room in a few long strides and intercepted her. He grabbed her with his one good hand, encircled her with his arms, and drew her to him. "Tillie, I know you believed me before the phone call, and I'm grateful for that."

She sank against him, feeling neither the will to resist nor the desire to pursue. "Of course, I believed you."

"I wish we could settle all the doubts between us as simply as that." His arms tightened. "I know we've been at odds. I admit I returned to Citrus County and to this company because I was worried about my mother's financial interests. But when you entered the picture, I saw that as soon as the time came when I could concentrate on my own interests, I would go straight to the girl I loved long ago."

A warm feeling of anticipation began to revive Tillie's spirits.

"Now I'll be able to do that."

"Do what?" She suddenly felt in a teasing mood.

He was still serious. "Develop my own interests, perhaps establish a real partnership."

"Not me. When I'm able to open my shop, I am doing it on my own."

He frowned. "I didn't mean a business partnership."

"You're looking for a partner?"

He lightly kissed her cheeks and forehead and parted her lips with his. Breathlessly she offered, "I know of someone who will soon be temporarily unemployed."

He grinned. "I want a partner who will commit for life. And," he added sternly, "she must be a Christian."

She considered that and eyed him wisely. "This person I'm speaking of might be just the partner for you. Not only is she a Christian, she's bright, witty, well read, and can even dodge rattlesnakes. . . ."

He stopped her with a kiss much longer than the first, one that told Tillie that every spark of their old love had survived.

When at last he released her, Tillie snuggled her head against his chest and murmured, "As I was saying when I was so rudely interrupted, this person is also interested in a lifetime commitment."

Austin gently caressed Tillie's face, tilting it toward his own, moving her lips closer and closer to his as he said softly, "Sounds like a perfect arrangement. Shall we shake on it?"

"No more handshake deals," she whispered. "But another kiss will do."

A Letter To Our Readers

Dear Reader:

In order that we might better contribute to your reading enjoyment, we would appreciate your taking a few minutes to respond to the following questions and return to:

Karen Carroll, Editor
Heartsong Presents
P.O. Box 719
Uhrichsville, Ohio 44683

1. Did you enjoy reading *Rebar*?
   ❑ Very much. I would like to see more books by this author!
   ❑ Moderately
   ❑ I would have enjoyed it more if

   _____

2. Where did you purchase this book? _____

   _____

3. What influenced your decision to purchase this book?
❑ Cover	❑ Back cover copy
❑ Title	❑ Friends
❑ Publicity	❑ Other _____

4. Please rate the following elements from 1 (poor) to 10 (superior).
   - ❑ Heroine   ❑ Plot
   - ❑ Hero   ❑ Inspirational theme
   - ❑ Setting   ❑ Secondary characters

5. What settings would you like to see in Heartsong Presents Books?

   _____

   _____

6. What are some inspirational themes you would like to see treated in future books?

   _____

   _____

7. Would you be interested in reading other Heartsong Presents Books?
   - ❑ Very interested
   - ❑ Moderately interested
   - ❑ Not interested

8. Please indicate your age range:
   - ❑ Under 18   ❑ 25-34   ❑ 46-55
   - ❑ 18-24   ❑ 35-45   ❑ Over 55

Name _____

Occupation _____

Address _____

City _____ State _____ Zip _____